MW01631859

WAITING FOR THE WHITE

And Other Tales From

Paul Estronza

Illustrated by

Waveland

to Carol Ann
Best Wishes and the
coast is waiting for your
Return
R. Estronza La Violette

PELICANS

The Mississippi Gulf Coast

La Violette

Patricia Rigney

Mississippi

WAITING FOR THE WHITE PELICANS

For reprint information contact:
laviolet@datasync.com

Published by Annabelle Publishing
Post Office Box 87
Waveland, MS 39576

Library of Congress Catalog Card Number:
00-191107

ISBN 0-9673936-1-2

Some of the tales in this book began their lives as Sunday columns in the *Sea Coast Echo,* a regional newspaper in Bay St. Louis, Mississippi.

Manufactured in Mississippi
Printed by Dolphin Press
987654321

First Edition

Front Cover
"White Pelican" by Patricia Rigney

Back Cover
The Author, his wife Stella and Gretal on Jeffrey's Pier, Christmas Day 1979.
Photograph by Albin J. Bielawski

TABLE OF CONTENTS

Table Of Contents
(Continued)

DEDICATION

To Leah Trealease, who long ago told me to keep going.

To the years of *WMCE a*nd to other memorable occasions that have made time pass in unusual ways: *Little Window, SUE, The Grand Banks* and *Donde Va?;*

To all of these and especially all the warm friends Stella and I have had the good fortune to gather as we passed by.

Other Books By Paul Estronza La Violette By Annabelle Publishing

---

Views From a Front Porch

Last year, Stella and I were standing on the porch looking somberly out over the tree-limbed debris left by Hurricane Georges. The hurricane had passed through the evening before. ...A shift in the predicted storm path had changed ...a complete catastrophe to just a lawn filled with debris ... our mind still clung to thoughts of catastrophe.

Stella suddenly pointed out towards the water to our east. There, just beyond the end of a neighbor's wooden pier, I saw a long line of about ten American White Pelicans flying impossibly low over the water ...

It had been fifteen years since Stella and I had last seen those large beautiful birds. That afternoon, the two of us were seeing them once more.

As we watched, the black-edged wings of the lead bird began a hard slow beat, raising the bird up from about a foot above the water to about eight or ten feet. There, its wings stopped their beat and remained motionless and the large bird began again a long, drawn-out, controlled gliding fall toward the water. Behind the lead, in an undulating wave, the other birds began their rise and fall in slow, exquisitely graceful ballet step.

They are indeed beautiful birds. ... If luck will have it in the years to come, Stella and I, together, will see them another time.

BAY OF
ST. LOUIS
GULFPORT
LONG BEACH
PASS CHRISTIAN
BAY ST. LOUIS
WAVELAND
MISSISSPPI SOUND
Cat Island
Ship Island
L. PONCHARTRAIN AND
L. BORGNE ←
GULF OF
MEXICO

PREFACE

This book contains vignettes of the life my wife, Stella, and I have led living in a town on the Gulf Coast of Mississippi.

It's a small town, one of the smallest of the string of coastal communities that line the northern shore of the Mississippi Sound. It's a friendly, comparatively quiet town and Stella and I have enjoyed the twenty-five years we've lived here. We have lived other places, but we've lived here the longest and we consider it our home.

We spent these years in a large, comfortable beach house that we both helped build. The house sprawls among several old live oaks, some of which are centuries old. To catch the cooling breezes, we built a wide, covered veranda that stretches around the house's south and west sides. This veranda is important in that much of the things I talk about in this book center on the view from the veranda.

The view through the thick trunks and branches of the old live oaks is extremely nice. About a hundred feet away from the house lay a two-lane county road with the rather pretentious name of Beach Boulevard. On the other side of this narrow road is a sandy man-made beach and beyond that, stretching in a large arc that dominates most of our view, are the tea-brown waters of the Mississippi Sound.

The Sound is an estuary, about a hundred or so miles long and ten to fifteen miles wide. This long, shallow estuary separates the Mississippi coast from the clear blue waters of the Gulf of Mexico. It forms a richly diverse mixing zone for the fresh waters that pour out of the coastal bayous, rivers and lakes and the more salty waters that intrude in from the Gulf.

Ours and the other towns on the coast are situated on the north side of the Sound. On the south side lies a long string of unpopulated, relatively untouched islands that are mostly national parks. These islands act as both a natural playground for us to enjoy and as a physical barrier that protects our coastal communities from the sometimes violent Gulf storms.

This biologically rich, long, shallow Sound is a ubiquitous part of our everyday life and its presence shapes much of the unique character of our coastal living.

In this book I talk about the Sound, about its birds, its fish, its beaches… I tell stories about the Sound and all of these as well as tales of how the Sound and they interact with our town and its people and those of the nearby coastal towns.

Almost always you will find the Sound forms a rich backdrop to the tales I tell of Stella's and my experiences in living in this sprawling beach house, miles from where both of us were born, here, in a small southern coastal town we now call home.

***

There is a lot in the stories that I have written here that include details of our lives with Jennie and Gretal and Lillie, our present and past Weimaranars, as well as Holly, our present and only black tomcat.

Stella and I have grandchildren and we love them. However, the animals I have written about here have been with us constantly. Jennie, Gretal, Lillie, and Holly have shared our days and nights, they have seen the same things we do and have offered to us their feelings on all of these.

They have done all this with a close love that has made our lives here far nicer than if they were not present. I ask therefore for an understanding and forgiveness if I seem to dwell too long on our association.

Finally, there is a "secret" to what I've written that I believe adds to the enjoyment of the stories.

I have tried to write each of the stories so that they may be easily read aloud to another person. Please try it. You'll find that you and the person you read it to will enjoy the stories a little bit more because of this.

At Heron Home
Waveland, Mississippi

The map on the following pages and the one facing the preface display most of the areas discussed in this book. These and all the maps that I have used have been modified from maps in Marine Resources and History of the Mississippi Gulf Coast Volume 2, *published by the Mississippi Department of Marine Resources. I strongly recommend this four volume set for any readers who wish more in-depth knowledge of the history and resources of the Mississippi Coast.*

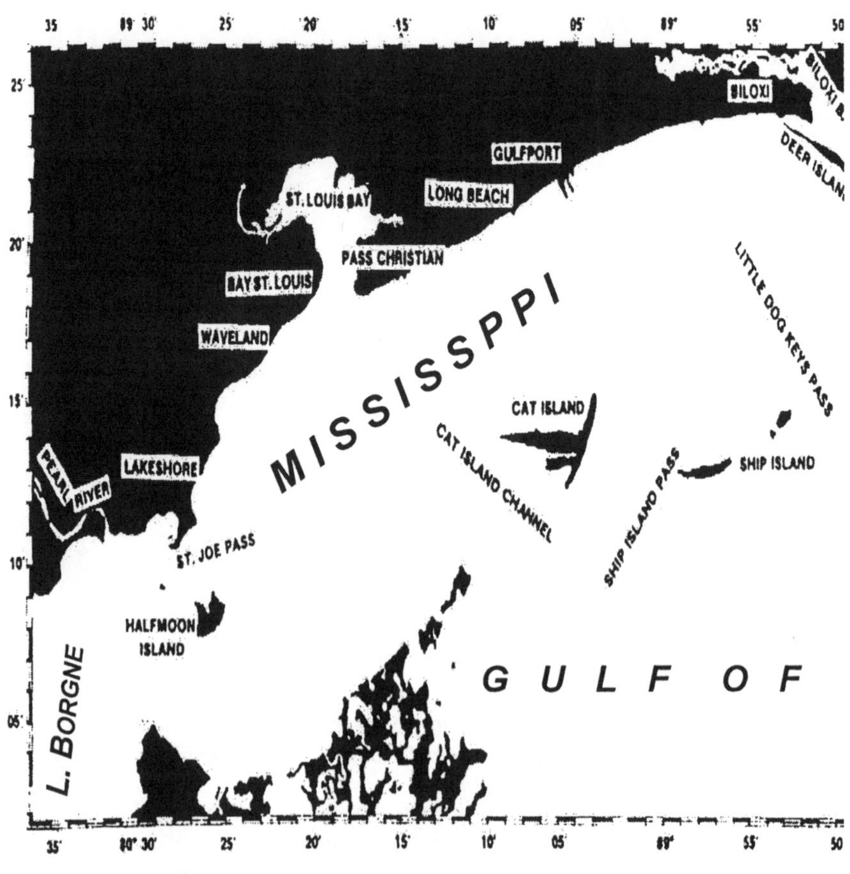
BILOXI
GULFPORT
LONG BEACH
ST. LOUIS BAY
PASS CHRISTIAN
BAY ST. LOUIS
WAVELAND
MISSISSPPI
CAT ISLAND
CAT ISLAND CHANNEL
LITTLE DOG KEYS PASS
SHIP ISLAND
SHIP ISLAND PASS
PEARL RIVER
LAKESHORE
ST. JOE PASS
HALFMOON ISLAND
L. BORGNE
GULF OF

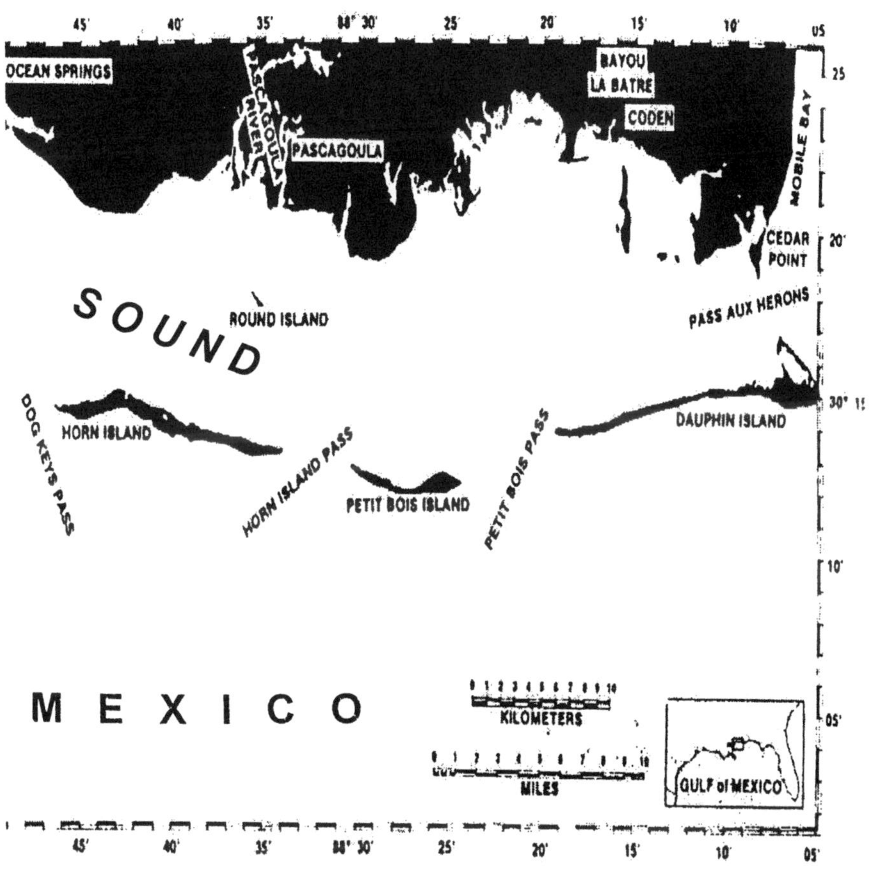
OCEAN SPRINGS
PASCAGOULA RIVER
PASCAGOULA
BAYOU LA BATRE
CODEN
MOBILE BAY
CEDAR POINT
SOUND
ROUND ISLAND
PASS AUX HERONS
DOG KEYS PASS
HORN ISLAND
HORN ISLAND PASS
PETIT BOIS ISLAND
PETIT BOIS PASS
DAUPHIN ISLAND
MEXICO
KILOMETERS
MILES
GULF of MEXICO

THE FIRST DAY OF SHRIMPING SEASON

...the dark clouds moving in add a harsh background to the colors of the scene and make a graphically splendid picture. Most of the boats are still in sun and well lit, but behind them there is blackness. ...There is a continuous shifting of the shrimp boats in front of this spreading mass of dark power, the boats moving about almost heedlessly as if they are automatons in a mindless pursuit of shrimp, unaware of the approaching menace...

It's June and today is the first day of shrimping season. Stretched across the horizon from west to east the shrimp boats are out in front of our house in force.

It's a large fleet; I hear estimates of 500 boats and that this is less than last year. Whatever the number, there are a lot of boats out there and they make an impressive show.

The string of towns along our coast are unusual in that, like coastal villages in the Mediterranean, each town has its own small fleet of shrimp and oyster boats. Our fleet is docked in various places along the shores of Bayou Caddy, whereas Pass Christian, Long Beach, and Gulfport have their fleets in their community marinas.

I'm taking a break from laying new dirt in the side garden and I've been sitting in the shade on the front porch to rest, drinking some sun tea and watching the show. It's a good show and, since it only comes once a year, I've decided to really stretch out and enjoy it.

I've seen the first day of shrimping season before and always my first question is how do they keep from running into one another? I feel like some type of macabre voyeur waiting to see some boat run across another boat's lines, but it doesn't happen.

It's early morning; not quite ten o'clock. I started moving the dirt at about seven to avoid the heat. The weather report says that it will reach up in the nineties today. Shoveling dirt is not very exciting and in this heat I prefer to sit and watch shrimp boats.

Stretched out in front me like this, the broad scene is like a gigantic screensaver on my computer, but the noise of the engines of all these boats belies any thought that this might be an illusion. This is real. There are a lot of boats out there and on those boats there are a lot of people working hard, very hard, to harvest the shrimp.

The boats do make a lot of noise. It's pervasive, blending into a broad hum that changes in pitch as the boats move about in front of me. It is far from a static scene; here there is a little clump of boats for a while, then they are gone and another clump forms over there. They move about as they work as if unsure where they should stay.

I see black clouds are starting to come in from the west. These are big clouds. Mean looking. The large fleet I see sprawled before me will have some rough going in about an hour. It shouldn't bother the large boats but it may give the smaller ones some trouble.

But from where I sit, these dark clouds add a harsh color of the scene and make a graphically splendid picture. As I watch, the clouds become more invasive. Most of the boats are still in sun and well lit, but behind them there is blackness. Even this blackness is not still; becoming gray, then black again as the clouds move forward.

There is a continuous shifting of the shrimp boats in front of this spreading mass of dark power, the boats moving about almost heedlessly as if they are automatons in a mindless pursuit of shrimp, unaware of the approaching menace.

As I was working in the yard a short time ago, a neighbor came by towing a small shrimp boat and yelled "did I want any shrimp?". I said yes and he pulled his truck and boat up by the side lawn. His face was beaming as he opened a couple of large coolers in the boat and showed me their contents. They were both filled with ice and shrimp!

They were nice shrimp and I gladly helped him cull out five pounds of shrimp for me to keep. As we did this, he told me about his morning's work. He had set two thirty-minute casts and had pulled in about one hundred- and-twenty pounds of shrimp.

This seemed impressive to me until he started to tell about the time he took to prepare, fuel, launch, get out, set up, turn around, get back, pull the boat out and return home. I figure that the whole thing equated to about a five-hour trip to get his two thirty-minute casts.

But he was happy and I guess that is what really matters. And looking at my shrimp, mixed, but about a thirty count (i.e., thirty shrimp to the pound), I'm happy, too. I pack them in a bucket of ice and water and put them in the refrigerator in the garage.

Many of the shrimpers out in the sound are like my neighbor, amateurs or semi-pros that go out only at the start of shrimp season or on weekends. As you drive along the back roads of Waveland, Shoreline Park or Claremont Harbor, each yard appears to have a small shrimp boat on a trailer.

Many of these small shrimpers keep a certain amount for themselves and unload the rest at a dock wholesaler or local middleman. Others sell their catches from the boat or have a local outlet. At this time of year you see small refrigerator trucks selling shrimp on the highway or hand-painted signs saying "Shrimp" and an arrow pointing to the back of somebody's house.

This rush to harvest the shrimp on opening day is very efficient. Perhaps too efficient.

Within two or three days the majority of the shrimp will have been removed from the Sound and the vast fleet I've been watching today will be gone three days from now (the season lasts from June through December).

The problem with this two- or three-day harvest is that the shrimp do not get a chance to get large and a good average counts range from 35 to 40 per pound

It’s too hot. I’ve quit trying to do any outside work and have gone back inside to the cool, quiet of my office. Jennie, my Weimaraner, likes this much better and has installed herself in her customary recess under my desk. I start typing as the naval clock I bought in Hamburg years ago strikes six bells; eleven o’clock. I decide I’ll work for another hour.

Looking out the office window I can still see the shrimp boats and, if I listen carefully, I can hear the muted sounds of their engines. But now there is another sound, intermittent, but when I hear it, it drowns out the noise of the boats.

It’s thunder.

The sound grows in volume with the gradual darkening of the sky. It seems to bloom out every few minutes in low rumbles that sometimes roll on in long, slowly diminishing echoes. Then silence, and then it starts again; each time it stops and starts it’s a little louder. It’s serious thunder and Jennie is starting to get nervous under the desk. Her nose touches my bare foot, a sign she is scared.

From my window, I can see some of the boats disappear behind a rapidly moving rainsquall; many are gone from sight altogether. Sheets of rain are starting to hit the house. Those boats that I can see however, have not stopped working. The men want their shrimp. The boats keep moving.

I wish them luck. Although I can see my shovel sticking out of the wet mound of topsoil in the yard, I'm not going back out today. I'm going to finish writing this and then go in the kitchen, make some coffee and see if there is any of Stella's pound cake left.

Stella's Pound Cake

1 pound butter (no substitute)
2 2/3 cups sugar
8 eggs, separated
3 ½ cups cake flour
½ cup whipping cream
1 teaspoon vanilla

Lightly grease a very large tube pan and set aside. Reserve 1/3-cup sugar for egg whites.

Cream butter thoroughly and add sugar gradually; continue to cream, beat about 10 minutes. Add egg yolks, one at a time, beat well after each addition. Sift flour 3 times; add alternately with the whipping cream and vanilla, beat for another 10 minutes until mixture is very light. Beat egg whites until frothy and then gradually add 1/3-cup sugar. Fold in by hand to creamed mixture.

Pour batter into tube pan and bake at 300° F for 1 and ¾ hours or until tests done. Let cool in pan for 10 minutes and then turn out and cool on rack.

(I like it plain, but it can be served with a lemon glaze. Plain goes especially good with fresh sweetened strawberries and whipped cream.)

SEAGULL, SEAGULL, ON THE WALL

...I have seen them follow a ship at sea for days far from land, riding the buffeted air created by the ship's turbulence. ... I've watched them soaring in a group of eight or ten gulls perfectly poised a little ways out from the side of the ship. There they would stay at rest, expending almost no energy, riding the ship's invisible stream of air. ...Then one day they are gone and we find we miss their presence, this tie to a shore we will not see for too, too long a time. ...

We have some interesting birds in our immediate area of the beach that make attention-getting displays.

During mating season, the Great Blue Herons put on particularly prominent displays when they stake out and defend territorial spaces in the shallows and on neighboring piers. And what's nice about all this is that, since much of these displays take place in front of our house, we get to watch.

Then there are other birds; seagulls, for example.

I've never been a big fan of seagulls. Oh sure, they have their adherents; "Jonathan Livingston Seagull" comes to mind as the all time sugary paragon of the good seagull. And if you go to any of the tourist shops in the Bay, seagulls predominate as the bird glorifying the watercolors they sell.

So there are people who like them.

To be truthful, we do have a rather nice watercolor of gulls on our dining room wall. I will admit the birds superficially look good in these pictures, but this may be because they are just photogenic and wear all those clean white feathers. I can never understand how they keep themselves so pristine white. I believe this whiteness is really a cover, a ruse. Because morally and in action, they are not squeaky clean by any stretch of the imagination.

From my own experience, seagulls are a noisy, quarrelsome, gregarious bunch of thieves with the capability – and evidently extreme strong desire – to whitewash an entire pier, dock or boat in one afternoon. In addition, they are rude, they are pushy and their laughter, to put it bluntly, is ridiculous.

As if all this wasn't enough, they argue incessantly.

It would seem that if one gull can't get along with the bird next to him, why doesn't he move to another part of the beach? No, it appears that it's easier for them to argue. And they do.

I asked Stella about this one day while we were sitting on the porch and a group of gulls were being particularly noisy on the beach in front of the house. She put her book down and watched them for a while. Finally she said, "I think they just like to argue."

***

Even among birds, I don't believe this life style is really necessary. Other beach birds don't exhibit the same behavior and appear to exist just as well.

For example, there is a group of sandpipers on our beach that are a pleasure to have about. They are also gregarious but, unlike the seagulls, they get along with each other very well. In fact, they seem to exemplify niceness. This wholesome togetherness is epitomized in their synchronized flying. They do this in small, tightly packed groups, flying just above the water.

As they fly they continuously keep together in seemingly impossible close order, the group turning rapidly as if one bird, showing themselves one moment as a cloud of brilliant white dots, then in another moment as an almost invisible gray cloud.

The flick, flick as their white and then gray sides are alternately turned to us in the late afternoon sun is a delight to watch. Conversely, seagulls seem to fly about in ever-changing groups of disorganized noisy rabble, yelling and calling each other names while landing and taking off as if each one wants to be boss.

If there is anything they seem to possess in abundance, it seems to be this general spirit of disorganization.

Nature is not casual. There is usually a reason for what we see around us. So, there must be a reason for this behavior, perhaps some Darwinian aspect to preserve their species. If so, it appears to work, because the world's supply of seagulls seems to be inexhaustible and there are times on our beach that there seems to be twice that amount.

They are good flyers, I will admit. I have seen them follow a ship at sea for days far from land, riding the buffeted air created by the ship's turbulence. Bad weather, good weather, they're there.

I've watched them soaring in a group of eight or ten gulls perfectly poised a little way out from the side of the ship. There they would stay at rest, expending almost no energy, riding the ship's invisible stream of air. Then, coming to life, they fly off to catch some fish or debris thrown from the ship.

Their swooping flights at these times call for a skillful integration of the ship's speed and the relative winds; both of which can have considerable variability. Watching them from the bridge as they resolve all these complex factors to snatch some potato peeling from the ship's wake, produces a mixed feeling of awe.

Then one day they are gone and we find we miss their presence, this tie to a shore we will not see for too, too long a time.

***

There are times when they can be lovely to watch on land as well. When I lie on the lounge on the porch, I can often see flitting glimpses of passing troops of gulls through gaps in the oak branches above me.

This is especially true when there is a strong wind. Like their brethren at sea, these shore gulls ride uplifting currents of air, their wings held gracefully out, unmoving except for slight angle shifts of their tip feathers. They exert almost no effort, drifting, drifting in long silent flight in a sea of air.

Lulled by the rhythm of their passage, I would lie back watching through the branches, as wave after wave of gulls flow by, in ones and twos, in fives, in tens, silent white ghosts riding the invisible wind.

One stormy afternoon, I sat in my dining room and watched a large flock of seagulls sitting on the beach along the water's edge. Winds and rainsqualls associated with a nearby Gulf storm had been pelting us since the day before. I could hear the wind and the tall thin windows on the west side of the room were obscured by hard sheets of gusting rain.

That morning the storm seemed to have been letting up, but by afternoon, it became obvious that that had just been a temporary lull and the winds and driving rains had started to intensify again. The sky on the horizon, especially to the southwest, had become dark; almost a black-blue, and I knew that heavier rains were due.

The strong winds, aided by a spring tide, had pushed on the waters in the Sound, pushing them higher on the beach than would a high spring tide. A long wrack line had formed on the newly laid sand berm formed by this excessive high water. Here and there behind the berm, I could see pools that had formed where the water had bypassed the new berm.

The gulls stood among the debris, their feet in water, their bodies hunched, faced into the direction of the driving rain. As I watched them sitting there, I thought of their motionless flights past the branches of my oaks and in the stronger winds beside the ship when I was at sea.

Perhaps as they sat there in the miserable wind and rain, their thoughts were of those moments also and they dreamed of other days.

On second thought, I believe seagulls are more pragmatic birds. More likely, they were just sitting there with the endless patience of such creatures; waiting numbly for conditions to change. To me as I watched them, they look like rugged survivors, birds that are every bit a part of stormy as well as sunny days.

When you think of it, this may well be their true beauty.

WAKEY! WAKEY! WAKEY! RISE AND SHINE![*]

...But I am doing something that is important to me, important in that otherwise I would have as easily stayed in bed for another hour or two. I'm absorbing in a subliminal way the rising of the new day. I'm very gradually letting in a conscious feeling of being alive. I don't think about this. I just let it slowly happen. Very slowly. And when it does, I'm ready. ...

I'm an early morning riser.

But this does not mean I'm totally awake when I rise. It takes awhile. I normally get up between six and six-thirty, shower and proceed to the kitchen. There, I fix coffee, orange juice, some toast, and a small dish of tapioca and then go sit on the porch or, if it's hot, in the dining room and watch the sun come up.

I do all this in a sort of comatose state, moving from task to task by force of habit. Jennie stays close behind me, following my staggering path even when I'm obviously confused on exactly where I'm supposed to go.

As I move about, I hear the nails of her paws clicking faintly on the Mexican tiles of the kitchen floor. They make a pleasant sound in the soft morning quiet of the house.

Sitting down finally for breakfast seems to ease my confusion. I then can just stare at the morning scene, the beach, the waters of the Sound, the gulls and the sun starting its rise. I'm not contemplating any world-shaking thoughts. Mostly, I'm just sitting, sipping my coffee, looking out on a world freshly touched by the new day's sun.

---

* Start of British Royal Navy reveille call

But I am doing something that is important to me, important in that otherwise I would have as easily stayed in bed for another hour or two. I'm absorbing in a subliminal way the rising of the new day. I'm very gradually letting in a conscious feeling of being alive. I don't think about this. I just let it slowly happen. Very slowly. And when it does, I'm ready.

I reach down and stroke Jennie sitting patiently beside me; I wave at a jogger going by on the beach road. I'm alive, I'm here, it's another day, and it feels good.

***

There are other people like me, people who get up early so that they'll have a longer time to loaf. But there are just as many other people who feel as strongly about the other end of the day – the time of sunset and the coming of night.

I had a delightful thing happen to me years ago that addressed both sides of our emotional relationship with the day's sunrise and sunset.

I had been working on an oceanographic research ship in the Indian Ocean and had gotten off when it docked at Mahe in the Seychelles Islands. From there I thought I would catch a plane back to Africa and then the States.

I quickly found that this wasn't easy. First there was only one plane, a small two-engine amphibian (there was no airport on the island in those days). Then when I inquired about it, I was told that the plane had developed some type of internal disorder that required major work.

"It's going to take about another two weeks or so," said the pilot, sitting moodily in a lawn chair on the dock staring at the plane in the water. "Get yourself a place at Marie's and we'll call you when we're ready to go to Mombassa."

When I made inquiries about Marie's, I found it was a small hotel located on the other side of the island and accessible only by a narrow winding road over the island's small mountain.

At Marie's, I found it was full of semi-permanent residents, mostly expatriates, and there was no room available. However, there was a small house just across the road from the hotel that was available for a short-time rental. I could stay there and arrange to have my meals at the hotel.

I loved the house when I saw it and immediately took it. It was really just a long set of several rooms set up on stilts on the beach itself. It had a long veranda on the water side with very comfortable porch furniture. I was told that the rising tide often flooded the under part and when this happened, I would have to wade to get to my tiny rental car.

In the early evening hours of the first day, I was surprised by visitors – a man and his wife from the hotel. We sat on the veranda of the house and enjoyed its breathtaking view of the Indian Ocean.

When my visitors placed a new bottle of gin whiskey on a side table, I got some ice and tonic and we proceeded to have a "Sundowner." We sat and looked over the water at a distant island, aptly called, Silhouette Island, and watched the sun make its magnificent daily plop into the sea.

It was a pleasant visit, the three of us sitting there, sipping our drinks, watching the sea, and making an occasional remark or two. However, an odd thing happened during the visit. The woman, and later the man, got up and stayed in the bathroom for what I considered an extraordinarily long time. Also, after they were gone, I found they had left the bottle of gin on the side table. It was good gin.

The next evening, another couple stopped by, enjoyed the sunset with me and left another bottle. Only this time it was a very nice scotch. Over the next week, this happened several times, each time a different couple. They were pleasant visits and I really couldn't complain.

Oddly enough, they all used the bathroom for long periods during their visits. I checked the bathroom after they left; everything seemed in order. Perhaps the room seemed a bit damp, but then I was on the water and there was no glass in any of the windows, only screens.

On Saturday, when I went shopping in Victoria, the main town on the island, a man turned to me at the grocers and asked if I was the fellow staying at the Kimble House at Marie's.

"Why, yes. I am," I said.

"Oh, very good!" he said "I wonder if you would mind if my wife and I stopped over, say tomorrow, and have a Sundowner with you?"

I was nonplussed, but agreed that that would be nice and he left. I turned to the clerk who was smiling at my puzzled face.

"When you rent the Kimball House, sir," he explained "you rent a house at the hotel with the only bathtub on the far side of the island. It is a very deep tub with lots of hot water. It is considered good manners to let the people on that side of the island use it during your stay."

"A bath?" I asked, amazed. "Don't they have showers?"

"But, sir. A shower cannot replace a good soak in a hot tub."

***

But that's just the one side of the day, the time of sunset. Let me tell about the earlier side. When I took the Kimble House, I was asked by the clerk at Marie's what time I wanted to be "knocked up" in the morning.

"What??"

"Morning tea, sir," he quickly said. "What time do you wish us to bring you your morning tea?"

I said six for no other reason than that was the time I usually woke up and thought that it would be nice to have tea then. The next day and all of the following days of my stay, I was awakened by the delightful vision of a young girl running lightly into my room with a tea tray in one hand and holding a black straw hat on her head with the other.

She was like a faint, almost ethereal, whirlwind. She would say good morning in the soft voice of the islanders, lay the tray down beside the bed and dash out, still holding her straw hat on her head.

I would get up, clutch a large cup of hot strong tea off the tray, stagger out on the veranda, listen to the birds in the tree next to the house and the surf only yards away, and slowly greet the day.

One day, I was stopped on the street in Victoria by a small boy who clutched my arm and told me, "The plane, sir, the plane is ready."

When I went to the harbor with him, I found the two-engine amphibian still floating squat in the water, but evidently cured of whatever mysterious ailment it had had. It really did not look all that reliable. But I had been gone from home for almost two months and it was time to head back.

The next day the plane took off with me aboard. It was Sunday and I remember watching the pilot say his rosary with a fervor that I wondered was either due to religious zeal or the condition of the plane. In any case, it was a wretchedly long and noisy nine-hour flight before we landed at the airport in Mombassa, Kenya.

Once there, I felt exhausted. I decided to treat myself to a stay at a five-star hotel. Nice as my stay at Marie's was, it lacked a number of amenities. I had some extra money and this seemed a good time to spend it.

The clerk seemed to sense what I wanted and suggested that perhaps I would like one of the guest cottages located in the broad, park-like gardens in the back of the hotel.

I had seen them when I arrived and they looked very nice. There was still the spirit of British colonialism about the place and the gardens and cottages gave the place an air of being very plush, plush.

I said I would take one.

He then asked me what time I would like my morning tea. Remembering the soft, quiet, almost wraith-like visits I had had each morning at Kimble House, I stood there for a moment, savoring the thought of experiencing a morning wake up one more time before going home.

I smiled and said, "Six."

The next morning, I was startled from my sleep by three heavy knocks on the carved wooden door.

When I groggily called out, "Come in," the heavy door swung abruptly open, a seven foot, 300 pound African in a splendidly brilliant hotel uniform strode heavily into the room, loudly placed an immense tea tray on my small table and, in a deep bass bellow that shook the walls of the small cottage, wished me a

"GOOD MORNING, SIR!!!"

WAITING FOR THE WHITE PELICANS[*]

...We often see a line of three or four birds flying low over the water. As their glide deteriorates, the line sinks slowly lower and lower toward the water, until finally the air beneath the leader can no longer support it. Then it flaps its wings hard several times and rises up to its previous height of about ten feet to start the glide anew. ...The second bird in line now feels the lack of air support and, with a hard flapping of its wings, it too rises to the height of the leader and joins its glide. Behind it the third bird in line flaps and rises and the fourth ... each bird rising in sequential step like a graceful syncopated line of ballet dancers. ...

It happened on a Sunday morning in spring.

As we were preparing to have coffee on the porch, Stella and I were startled to see what appeared to be about twenty large white life jackets floating high in the shallows over by Carrere's pier, a long wooden pier located about 400 yards west of our house.

We were puzzled. Our first thoughts were that a boat had overturned further out in the Sound and these jackets had washed in, trapped in the lee eddy set up by the pier. However, the "jackets" appeared to be too big, too white, too many.

Then they began to move.

---

[*] Modified from a chapter in *Views From a Front Porch*

Several cars on the beach road in front of our house slowed. Some stopped completely and rolled their windows down as the people inside stared out. Several got out of their cars and stood on the edge of the road and watched. We phoned two of our neighbors and they came and joined us and we all watched with binoculars hurriedly brought out from inside the house.

The floating objects were American White Pelicans, huge birds with wings that can span more than nine feet!

The large birds stayed where they were, mostly sleeping, for perhaps an hour, ignoring the to-do of the increasing number of people who had gathered to watch from the road and beach. Then, suddenly, with a noisy rush of wings, they lifted and, as a group, flew away.

Although I'm told American White Pelicans are around the coastal area, they stay in more protected waters to feed. It would be years before Stella and I would see the American Whites again.

***

That afternoon, I called Stella to come out and join me on the porch and to bring out the binoculars. I pointed to the water. Together we counted eleven Brown Pelicans perched on pilings in the water in front of us.

There had not been any there the day before, nor the day before that, nor the week before. *In fact, we had not seen a pelican, Brown or White, in the five years we had lived on the Coast.* What we were seeing was a resurgence of a species that had almost become extinct.

In the following weeks, more Brown Pelicans came and went, their number steadily increasing, until finally it seemed that every piling we could see had its own birds. The Brown Pelicans were back and in such numbers that they were obviously here to stay.

I remember that wonderful summer in 1983, as the year the Brown Pelicans reestablished themselves as an integral part of our coastal scene.

***

To be truthful, I had never thought too much of pelicans in the years I spent at sea. To me, they were just another of the birds present when the ship docked, and, although not noisy like seagulls, they were the trite subject of souvenir beach shops, displayed sitting on posts with bits of nautical-looking rope wrapped around their bases. In those commercial displays, they were seldom shown in flight and, if they were, the presentation had a bland, an almost static dullness.

There is even a whimsical poem that makes the bird seem to be a bit of a clown: "A wonderful bird is the pelican, / His bill can hold more than his belly can ...".

The result of all of this to me and, I suppose, to a lot of people was that pelicans appeared to be an ungainly bird, almost ugly. But now as I watched them in front of our home, I found that I had been badly mistaken. They are far from being ugly and certainly not ungainly; they are beautiful birds with an inherent wonderful grace in their movements that is a joy to witness.

I found they are their most graceful when they are in flight.

I would see a pelican skimming impossibly low over the water, and except for slight feather corrections, remaining motionless. The bird would be falling, but falling in a long, drawn out, perfectly controlled manner, floating on a weakening cushion of air, that held the bird as it glided on and on, sinking lower and lower towards the water.

Then at the last possible moment, when that final bit of air was all but gone, the bird would catch itself and, with several hard flaps of its wings, rise up above the water to eight to ten feet, where it again would begin its long, beautifully graceful, skimming, controlled glide.

Sometimes I would watch one pelican flying low over the water, and this is lovely to see. But for true grace, it's best to watch them "drafting" one another to minimize air resistance, flying in a linear loose staggered formation, en echelon.

I would often see a line of three or four birds flying low over the water. As their glides deteriorate, the birds would slowly sink lower and lower toward the water, until finally the air beneath the leading bird could no longer support it. Then it would flap its wings hard several times and rise up to its previous height of about ten feet and there it would start its glide anew.

The second bird in line now feels the lack of air support and, with a hard flapping of its wings, it too would rise to the height of the leader and renew its glide. Behind it the third bird in line would then flap and rise and then the fourth … each bird rising in sequential step like a graceful syncopated line of ballet dancers.

When they fly high, they usually do so in a line of ten or more birds, the group undulating behind the lead bird in beautifully graceful waves. We often see such formations as we go down Highway 90, the beach road to Biloxi. In these formations the birds follow the road for long distances, riding the coastal sea breeze.

The uplift of the breeze holds them aloft some thirty feet above the road, so that they no longer really need the draft of the lead bird. As a result their formations are more loose and their wings remain almost motionless in a kind of hunkered outstretch to catch the lift.

They ride noiselessly in their flight; dark silhouettes, drifting across the road in long graceful back and forth sweeps, ignoring the near-accidents below as drivers such as myself, entranced by their passing beauty, crane their heads to watch.

There is even a festiveness about the way Brown Pelicans fish. Normally they do this in loose groups, hovering about ten to twelve feet over the water, making short sweeps before one, then another, and then another, drop as stones toward the water.

And as stones, they hit hard, sending up small eruptions of water. When a group of them find a good school of fish to work, it is like watching a bunch of small boys doing "cannonball" dives in a swimming pool with the almost continuous eruptions of water.

There is confusion about what actually happens when the birds dive, so each bird's drop must be watched rather carefully to see what really takes place. Each dive is slightly different, with the one constant being each bird's concentration on the fish that it is diving to catch.

As they fly, they search for fish just below the water's surface. Once a fish is targeted, the bird dives. In diving, the head of the bird remains rigidly oriented toward the fish it has targeted. The result is that the rest of the bird sometimes twists in a tight spiral as it falls to keep this orientation.

This committed concentration by the pelicans on their targets means that their original flight momentum will often turn their bodies in awkward angles to the water. The result is the sharp explosions that often occur when they hit the water surface. But when the water clears, there floating in the water, is a pelican with a fish cached in the large pocket of its bill.

The bird will sit for several moments, extending its neck up, downing its prey in large pulsing gulps, and then with slow massive flaps of its wings push itself up in the air again to join the others of its fishing group in their hunt for more fish to eat.

***

Last year, Stella and I were standing on the porch looking somberly out over the tree-limbed debris left by Hurricane Georges. The hurricane had passed through the evening before.

It had been a terribly heart-rendering two days for us. Only then were we really beginning to feel that our house and all we had and loved had been spared. Our thoughts as we looked out over the debris and toward the Sound were mixed. A shift in the predicted storm path had changed what could have been a complete catastrophe to just a lawn filled with debris. Although the lawn in front of us held comparatively minor debris, in our mind, we still clung to thoughts of what could have been a complete catastrophe.

Stella suddenly pointed out towards the water to our east. There, just beyond the end of a neighbor's wooden pier, I saw a long line of about ten American White Pelicans flying impossibly low over the water, their wings seemingly just missed touching the water.

It had been fifteen years since Stella and I had last seen those large beautiful birds. That afternoon, the two of us were seeing them once more.

As we watched, the black-edged wings of the lead bird began a hard slow beat, raising the bird up from about a foot above the water to about eight or ten feet. There, its wings stopped their beat and remained motionless and the large bird began again a long, drawn-out, controlled gliding fall toward the water.

Behind the lead, in an undulating wave, the other birds began their rise and fall in slow, exquisitely graceful ballet step.

They are indeed beautiful birds.

To us on that day they appeared as omens of what lay ahead. If luck will have it in the years to come, Stella and I, together, will see them another time.

THE LOUISIANA SHRIMPER

...I was greeted by a man in rubber boots standing by the boat's gunwale drinking a Barq's root beer. He was in his late twenties, pleasant looking, heavy-built but short, about five-seven, with big, obviously hard-worked hands. His most striking feature was a moon face that seemed to have a nice smile permanently carved in it. ...

On the eve of the start of the white shrimp season, my wife and I drove our granddaughter, Lorelei, over to Bayou Caddy to look at the shrimp boats docked there.

Lorelei wanted to see a working shrimp boat up close. She was from Michigan and here on her annual summer visit. We had taken her on the Biloxi shrimp boat ride and, although somewhat geared for tourists, the ride was nice and informative and it piqued Lorelei's interest.

Seeing her fascination with the process, I suggested that we take her to see the real thing. Each of the towns on the coast has its own shrimping fleet. Our local fleet is docked in Bayou Caddy, so it seemed to me to be the logical place to take her.

When we got to Bayou Caddy, we found a Louisiana boat by the dock that had just been loaded with ice. I got out of the car and walked over to the edge of the dock to ask if it was all right for Lorelei and Stella to take pictures.

I felt a little foolish.

I had been living down the road from Bayou Caddy for twenty-something years and had bought who knows how many pounds of shrimp from Bayou Caddy shrimpers and here I was asking if we could take pictures.

I was greeted by a man in rubber boots standing by the shrimp boat's gunwale drinking a Barq's root beer. He was in his late twenties, pleasant looking, heavy-built, but short, about five-seven, with big, obviously hard-worked hands. His most striking feature was a moon face that seemed to have a nice smile permanently carved in it.

We exchanged a few remarks and, for the sake of conversation, I asked him if he was headed out to catch the white shrimp. I felt reluctant to come right out and ask him if we could take pictures.

"Yes, sir." He had a soft, slow spoken, almost monotone, Louisiana drawl. "I've iced up and I'm going out in a few minutes. Be sitting right outside Bay St. Louis when the season starts tomorrow morning."

I made a couple more remarks and he, evidently feeling that our conversation might be a little prolonged, politely climbed up on the dock to stand by me.

He seemed proud of his boat and went through a lot of trouble to explain some of the working gear on the large afterdeck. Besides the required turtle-excluder gear, he had a device to limit the amount of by-catch in his hauls. By-catch is the assorted fish and whatnot hauled in by the net in addition to the shrimp. The shrimpers often sell the fish and throw the trash back over the side. It provides a little extra money and some shrimpers count on it.

"Culling the by-catch takes too much time," he explained. "It really ain't worth it and I'm going to be too busy to mess with it anyhow."

As I listened to what he was saying, I began to look more closely at the boat. It was a well kept boat, painted a bright white and it gleamed in the late afternoon light.

I was struck by the fact that everything was clean and trim, with very little loose gear on the deck. Everything had a neat, almost formal look to it, as if the boat was getting ready for the annual blessing of the shrimp fleet.

I looked up at the large nets looming over us, jutting out from their masts on each side of the boat. Their size and the fact there were two trawls impressed me. I slowly realized that this was a good-sized boat and it carried some big gear and he had used the singular in referring to his next day's shrimping.

"Are you going out alone?" I asked.

"Yep, I usually go out with my brother, but he got sick with cancer a little while back. He suffered a bit for a long time and, well, last week he died. He and I always went out ever since I got the boat seven, eight years ago. Now I guess I'll do it alone."

I didn't know exactly what to say to this and gave what I hoped were the proper sympathetic remarks.

It was quiet for a few moments and I looked back to where Stella and Lorelei were standing by the car.

Trying to politely change the subject, I asked, "Can my wife and my granddaughter come over and take some pictures of your boat before you go out? My granddaughter is really interested in how you catch shrimp."

"Why, sure," he said nodding. "Be proud to have them." I waved and Stella came over with Lorelei, who, in typical teenage fashion, began asking a million questions. He patiently answered them all in his slow drawl.

Stella took a few pictures as she listened to the two talk and then stopped and looked around once more. She had also noticed his use of the singular and interrupted Lorelei's nonstop questions to ask him the same question I had asked him.

"Are you going out by yourself?"

"Yes, ma'am," he said and repeated in his matter-of-fact way the story about his brother. "He were the person who could just about guess where the best place to be to catch the shrimp. Seems like he just knew." He stopped talking for a moment and looked out over the boat.

"I'm going to miss him," he said. "We always worked good together, he and me. He was my best friend. Maybe I'll get a deckhand to help out later. I don't know. If that don't work out, I guess I'll sell."

Afterwards, he stood with Lorelei a little way down the dock and I took their picture with the big shrimp boat in the background, Lorelei all alive with a big smile and him standing a few inches taller in his rubber boots and pleasant face with its quiet built-in smile. Then we left.

Looking back as we drove off, I could see he had started his engine and was busy casting off from the dock.

I found a place to park by the channel entrance and the three of us got out. Standing there, we all waved and watched as the late sun lit up the bright white boat passing us with its one-man crew and memories of two.

I wish him well.

THE WEDDING GUEST

> ... *"Everything was new to me. I had to learn so many things, so very many things. ... "I learned to ride and I would go out with John and the men and sometimes we would stay for several days working the fence line and sleeping under the stars. We really didn't have to but we did because it was so... Oh, I really don't know how to describe the feeling."* ...

It was a beautiful day for a wedding.

Stella and I were over in Pass Christian to see some friends get married. When the music began and the bride came down the aisle, the brightness of the spring day poured into the church. The clean, crisp sunlight was the icing on the cake that made everything seem perfect. I like weddings and I leaned back in my seat and relaxed and enjoyed this one.

Later, at the reception we sat at a table with some friends. Almost immediately someone asked Stella to dance and quickly the other two couples at the table were up and dancing as well. Not to be outdone, I turned to the women sitting beside me and asked her if she would like to dance. She smiled and said no thank you.

She had a pleasant smile and I realized I didn't know her; she was a friend of one of the other couples. She was an older woman in her late seventies or early eighties. We exchanged a few remarks as we sat together and watched the people dancing.

"I really would like to dance," she volunteered almost wistfully after a minute, "but I twisted my knee in the garden yesterday and I'm afraid to aggravate it any more."

"May I have the first dance at the next wedding?" I asked.

"Of course," she said and gave me the pleasure of seeing her smile again. "May I have your name for my dance card?" I gave it to her and she pantomimed writing it down and then introduced herself. With this we were soon deep in one of those curiously intimate conversations strangers have who meet briefly and never see each other again.

I told her how Stella and I came to live on the Mississippi Gulf Coast and about my children and grandchildren in other states. In the telling, I mentioned several things that I usually don't tell people. In turn, I asked her about herself.

"I'm from here," she said. "I've lived here most of my life. I taught in the school system for a long time." In answer to my next question, she said that she never married during that time, as she had to take care of her mother.

"It's an old story," she said with a trace of bitterness. "Everyone else had families to take care of and I didn't, so I was the so-called logical one. Of course, while she was alive I couldn't marry. Who would have me?"

"Then she's dead?" I asked.

"Yes, she died when I was fifty-five. I was lost on what to do with myself for a year. Then a wonderful man came to visit on the Coast for the summer. He started to take me out. We would go to New Orleans or over to Alabama to Bellingrath Gardens. We went to places I had always wanted to go to, but never would.

"Oh! Were my sisters ever upset. Especially when in September, when it came near for the time he was to leave, he asked me to marry him! He had a ranch in Sheridan, Wyoming and he wanted me to go back with him."

"Sheridan?" I said. "I did a field trip there when I was in college years ago. I liked it. Did you say yes?"

"Yes, I did, to everyone's surprise, including myself. Again, all my relatives tried to talk me out of it, but we got married anyway. It was a small ceremony, not like this," she waved her hand to take in the large hall and the many guests. "But it was beautiful. He was only a year older than me and we went to live on his ranch and, Oh! Paul, it was every bit as wonderful as he said it would be.

"It was a horse ranch," she said smiling in the remembrance. "We did have some cattle and it was fair size as the ranches around there went. The first winter was mild so I had a chance to get used to it and go out and make friends. You've been out there so you know how friendly people there can be. In a little while it was like I had always lived there. The second winter was fairly hard, but I loved it.

"Everything was new to me. I had to learn so many things, so very many things. What was wonderful was that I found I could do many of these new things.

"I learned to ride and I would go out with John and the men and sometimes we would stay for several days working the fence line and sleeping under the stars. We really didn't have to but we did because it was so… Oh, I really don't know how to describe the feeling."

She stopped for a moment and stared out at the dance floor seeing a place many miles and years away. Despite the noise of the party, it seemed quiet. I found that she was sitting so I could see out the window behind her. As I waited for her to continue, I looked out.

From where I was sitting, I could see the beach and the bright sunlit waters of the Mississippi Sound. A group of pelicans was working the water a little way out and I could see the splash as they dove after fish.

"How long did you stay out there?" I asked after a minute had gone by and she had not spoken. She looked at me as if she were coming up from some deep pool then turned and looked out the same window I had been looking through. I doubt if she saw the same things I had seen.

"It was a little over twenty-one years. Twenty-one years! They were wonderful years and John was a wonderful person to spend them with. I found that I really couldn't fault the life I had had before if at the end I had a chance to meet and marry someone like him.

"Oh, things weren't always perfect. But the times of good far outstripped the times of bad. Everything we did together seemed as if we should have been doing them all our lives.

"John had a slight heart problem. He took his medicine religiously, but one day he had a stroke while out in the back area. By the time we got a truck out there and got him into town it was too late.

"I did my best to run the place for about a year, but it was too much for me. His son by his first wife came down from the Dakotas with his family to help.

"I could see that the son really loved the place; that was where he had been born and raised. I felt after a bit that I didn't belong, that I was really a fifth wheel. I felt the ranch was rightly his by inheritance and I sold it to him for a small sum and came back here."

"How long ago was that?" I asked.

"Let me see. I'm eighty-two now. So that was five, almost six, years ago." She reached forward and took her Champagne glass and sipped it. "It was as if I had never left here. My sisters and everyone else treat me like I've barely survived a dreadful experience. I've tried telling them of what it was like, but they have never been there; they have no feeling of anywhere else but here."

She twirled the glass, swirling the small amount of Champagne in it and then drank it, grimacing at some thought, and placed the empty glass on the table.

"One day," she continued, "I suggested that I take the children horseback riding. My brother-in-law was horrified and absolutely refused letting them go with me. The thought that I could lead an outing like that was beyond him.

"They act like I'm so old when I am around them and I don't feel like I really am. I feel frustrated and confused. I really don't know what to do."

We were interrupted by the dancers as they came back full of the excitement and the fun of the occasion. All the noise of the room seemed to flood back over us and the brief feeling of isolation I had felt as the two of us talked was gone. We were no longer alone. Stella chastised me for not dancing and my new friend came to my defense, saying that I had been kind enough to stay and keep her company.

Then there was a lot more noise and, as the band struck up the regal Mardi Gras tune "If I Ever Cease to Love," the bride and groom entered the reception hall. The bride was beautiful and the groom had an embarrassed, but happy look of unexpected happiness.

We all stood up and applauded. My new friend stood next to me and I knew the few moments we had had together were slipping away.

"At least," I said, "you had the twenty-one years."

Her answer came in a low voice. With all the noise and bustle in the room as the bride and groom paraded in a broad circle keeping time to the music and applause, I almost missed it.

"Oh! Paul! Those twenty-one years went by so fast."

THE CAR WAVE

...It's really a nice friendly act; a social exchange among friends, a sort of "I see you" gesture. It has endless variations and nuances and, to be truthful, we actually enjoy it. ...

There was a honk and I turned and waved.

"Who was that?" asked Stella pulling her head out of the car trunk. We were in the Sav-A-Center parking lot and Stella and I were putting our groceries in the car.

I looked after the pickup moving away and finally turning up one of the lanes to leave the parking lot. "I don't know. I didn't recognize the truck and I couldn't see through the tinted windows." Stella looked after the pickup and shook her head. She didn't recognize it either.

The car wave or honk is a ritual on the Coast that isn't lightly ignored.

We live on the beach road and, since there is a lot of traffic, we are heavily involved in this ritual. If we are sitting on the porch or working in the garden and a car goes by and honks, our hands go up as if they are attached to strings. Without any thought involved, we wave.

Honk – wave, honk – wave; it has become such a reflex gesture that I find my hand twitches when I hear a horn while driving my pickup.

I'm not complaining. It's really a nice friendly act; a long distance "touch" between friends, a sort of comfortable, reassuring "I see you" gesture. It's a social exchange that has endless variations and nuances and, to be truthful, we actually enjoy it.

We look, for example, to the passage on Sunday mornings of two friends giving us a majestic wave and honk from their antique Rolls Royce "Silver Cloud" as they go by. We wave dutifully back.

They feel happy and we feel happy. It's that sort of thing.

However, the exchange has built in problems. The gesture is best, when you are able to see the person you are waving at. Sometimes, as in the Sav-A-Center parking lot, this can be rather hard.

It is a little confusing when we have no idea of who the people are or we don't recognize the car, or worse, not sure of which of several cars going by had honked or even be sure the honk was intended for us. With the dark tinted windows that are common here in the bright sunshine of the Coast, this happens more often than one would ordinarily think.

This ritualistic salute to friends, sometimes people you may have been talking to only a few hours before, seems to be an ingrained trait among us. I'm sure there are social researchers who know the exact derivation of the wave, but my opinion is that it is a remnant of an old military tradition, which shows peaceful intentions between possible combatants or the respect between combatants and non-combatants.

As a young seaman standing bridge watch on a Navy destroyer, I remember witnessing our ship return the salute of a passing merchant vessel. As the merchant came abreast of our ship, I saw a small figure dash aft from the merchantman's bridge and lower the ship's national flag. Once their flag was down, we quickly dipped our colors up and down in a sort of superior acknowledgement. Then their flag was run up again and the small figure returned on the run to the bridge.

It was a pretty ceremony to see take place and a very close kin to the social wave I'm talking about here.

Because if, heaven forbid, Stella or I don't acknowledge a wave for some reason, I'm sure a shot will be fired across our bow the next time we meet our injured friend.

"Boy, I tell you, Mister Paul, you and Miss Stella must be mighty busy to not even..."

***

When we extended the garage, the concrete had to be wheel barrowed in. It was hard work and the contractor hired some muscular laborers to do the wheel barrowing. One of the laborers who did this came by a few weeks later. He was looking for some extra work and asked if there was anything that I might need done around the property on Saturday.

To be truthful, there is always something that needs to be done. I'm a terrible procrastinator on any job that looks like it might involve heavy work.

I said, "Sure."

He came that Saturday and I was happy to find that we worked well together. By the end of the day we had accomplished a surprising amount of work. There was still a lot of things to do, however, so he came back the next Saturday, and then the next, and the one after that, until Charles became a regular part of our Saturday routine.

It became our custom for Charles to sit with me at lunchtime in the gazebo. Stella would hear us washing up in the sink in the garage and, by the time we were seated in the gazebo, she would bring out huge po'boy sandwiches, a pitcher of iced sun tea and join us.

It was a great way to split the middle of a busy Saturday. We'd sit, watch the water, eat the po'boys, drink the tea, wave at the cars going by and listen to Charles tell us stories about Waveland politics.

Charles worked for the Municipality of Waveland in what was at that time the town-owned Sanitation Department. We quickly discovered there were several very nice perks to having this tie to the town government. Besides hearing stories about the town politics, which were often hilarious, Charles saw to it that we had the best picked-up garbage in Waveland.

Charles taught me that there were many types of waves.

Whenever I drove him home after he was done on a Saturday, he would return the waves of his friends that we passed. Only his wave was different, much different, almost regal.

He waved with a slow, short, barely wrist bending motion: almost an unperceivable nod of his hand. It was beautiful gesture and I was envious.

I practiced it and practiced it. Then I tried it one day when I passed some friends in front of Sav-A-Center. I thought I had it right, but unfortunately, I had Stella with me in the pickup.

She turned, looked back at the people, and then back at me and shook her head.

I haven't done it since.

BUT IT'S NOT THURSDAY IN KOREA

...I discovered the watch's date indicator. It and the weekday window showed the date and weekday in Korea. I decided that rather than running the risk of activating the bells again – I wasn't sure how I had deactivated them – I would just subtract a day when I used the window or referenced the date. This seemed the easiest approach.

I bought a new watch while I was in Korea.

We were back in Pusan after an extremely cold and stormy winter cruise in the northern Sea of Japan. We would be there four days unloading our instruments before heading back to Mississippi. It was both Sunday and Chinese New Year and I had taken the day off to shop the street vendors who lined the sea front area of the city.

"15,000 wan," said the vendor.

"14,000," I countered.

"No, no, 15,000"

It was obvious that he wasn't going to budge. I needed a watch. My old watch's crystal was scratched and I had been having difficulty reading the time. 15,000 wan was about $13. The watch looked good and at that price seemed a good buy.

The watch the vendor was showing me was battery operated, waterproof, and had five large buttons to work the various programs and a stainless steel, very macho case.

I was especially impressed when I pressed the button for the night-light. It was extremely bright. Its dial was also impressive, showing a large digital display with three mysterious windows in the upper half of the dial.

"What are the three windows for?" I asked. The vendor consulted with his companion and after a great deal of discussion, he wrote something down on a piece of paper and then, after checking it with his companion, handed it to me.

He had written, "15,000 wan."

I nodded and bought the watch, making sure he put the instructions in the plastic watchcase.

At the hotel the next morning, my roommate, Bob, looked up from his breakfast sweet roll. "I see you have a new watch."

I showed it to him. "Looks good," he said after examining it. "What are the three windows for?" I dug the instructions out from my wallet and looked at them. The print was very small and appeared to be written in English, French and Korean. I had a hard time reading the tiny print and handed it to him.

"Paul," he said after looking at the paper, "doesn't your watch have five buttons?"

"Yes," I said.

"Then they gave you instructions for the wrong watch. This diagram shows only four buttons and I don't see anything about the three windows."

I took the instructions back and looked at the diagram. He was right; it showed only four buttons!

"Well, anyway," I said. "It was a good buy."

"Not if you can use it for only three days," he said getting up and getting ready to leave for the ship. "Remember, we're going back home tomorrow. How are you going to change it to Mississippi time without instructions?"

"I'll figure it out."

He nodded and, as we both began to leave the hotel, he said, "By the way, don't keep looking at your watch when you're in bed tonight."

"Why not?"

"That night-light lights up the whole room," he replied. "Every time you checked the time last night, you woke me up."

***

When I got back to Mississippi, I showed the watch to Stella and explained my problem.

"I figure these kinds of watches are all probably generic," I said, "The instruction for one probably fits all." I then got the instructions out and asked her to read them aloud to me while I adjusted the time.

She puzzled over the small print and then started reading them aloud in a singsong voice, "To adjust time, depress 1 and hold 2 to fix time without changing day rate. Alternating 1 and 2. This will speed the adjustments for the multiple uses…"

"What?"

"That's what it says," she said looking up from the paper. "I think you wasted $15."

"It was 15,000 wan, not $15. Let me see that."

It was as she had read it to me. I glanced at the French. My French is poor, but even I could see it made no better sense than the English instructions. I turned it over and looked at the Korean hieroglyphics.

"That's Korean," Stella said. She had been watching me silently mouth the French instructions. I glared at her and she picked up her book and ignored me.

When I was alone the next morning, I started to experiment with the buttons. I felt that I had begun to make sense out of the three windows. Since the time I had bought the watch, I had noticed that there had been movement in two of the windows.

The first appeared to indicate the day of the week by a dot on a circle. This now indicated that in Korea, it was a day later in the week than it was in Mississippi. The second showed a small moon at the quarter stage. When I had been in Korea, it had been a new moon and the window, correctly, had been blank. The third window was still empty.

Finally, after much experimenting, I did get it changed to local Mississippi time. I should have been happy, only now I noticed that a large bell had appeared in the third window.

Sure enough at three that afternoon, the alarm went off. I managed to stop it, but noticed I had put the watch in the twenty four-hour mode. It now read 1500 hrs. I worked on both problems and managed to get back to a twelve-hour mode. The bell in the third window was now smaller. What did that mean?

On the half hour, I found out when the watch gave an annoying chirp. It was now programmed to go off every half hour day and night.

I wrestled with the buttons some more and managed to get the bell to disappear and the time to stay in the twelve-hour mode. In doing all this, I discovered the watch's date indicator. It and the weekday window showed Korean date and weekday.

I decided that rather than running the risk of activating the bells again – I wasn't sure how I had deactivated them – I would just subtract a day when I used the window or referenced the date. This seemed the easiest approach.

That night I told Stella what I had done, but not saying anything about the date problem. She nodded noncommittally. Later when I took Jennie outside, I stood on the porch and looked up at the moon low in the sky over the waters of the Sound. I called Stella outside and pointed to the moon.

"See what stage it's in?" I said proudly. "Now, look at my watch." With that I pushed the night-light and she looked at the tiny quarter moon in the middle window. Then she looked up again at the bright near half moon hovering over the water.

"But the moon is almost at the half," she said. "Maybe it's just a quarter moon now in Korea."

"Its not quite half. It probably changes when it is exactly at the half moon phase."

She gave me the same nod that Bob had given me. I was glad I had not told her about the dates. She turned and called Jennie who was watching us from the lawn.

"Lets go back in, it's cold," she said. "And, please, stop pressing that night-light. It's so bright, it's scaring Jennie."

I'm keeping the watch. It's a good watch. I don't care if it's not Thursday in Korea.

THE SEASONS ON THE MISSISSIPPI GULF COAST[*]

Stella's Lemon Ice for Summer

2 tsp. lemon rind *2 cups sugar*
4 cups water *¼ teaspoon salt*
3/4 cup lemon juice (fresh, not bottled)

Grate lemons onto sugar. Add water and salt. Heat slowly until sugar dissolves. Bring to a boil and boil for five minutes, covered without stirring to avoid crystallization. Chill and then add lemon juice. Churn or still freeze. A surprisingly excellent alternative is fresh grapefruit juice. Both are extremely refreshing.

Summers last longer here on the Coast than they do farther north. They aren't necessarily hotter, but the heat is spread over a longer period of time of the year and it seems hotter.

Luckily, our being close to the waters of the Mississippi Sound tends to mitigate the higher temperatures. In fact, the history and growth of Waveland and Bay St. Louis at the end of the last century hinged on this fact. In the years that followed the Civil War, it became a resort area.

---

[*] Modified from *Views From a Front Porch*

A fast and efficient rail service between Mobile and New Orleans was completed in 1870 and created quite a change.

Before this, it took an all day journey to get to the Coast. The visitors from New Orleans that came for the summer, took a train from the city to Lake Pontchartrain and then boarded a steam packet to the Coast towns.

But once here, the families would spend the whole summer away from the miasma of the city, taking advantage of the "balmy breezes and the good coastal airs."

All this changed when the fast trains made it possible to travel the 50 miles from New Orleans to Waveland and the Bay in an hour. Now, in addition to the summer visitors, people would come for just the day or to spend the entire weekend.

A new urban aspect was introduced to the area, the commuter.

The trains ran schedules that allowed businessmen to leave their families on the Coast and commute each day to New Orleans if they wished.

They could board their "club car" in Bay St. Louis at 8:00 a.m., and in Waveland minutes later, have a leisurely breakfast en route, and debark at Canal Street an hour later. In the afternoon, they would board the train at 4:00 p.m. and arrive at the Waveland and Bay stations at around 5:00 p.m.

The area quickly became a fashionable place to go to escape the New Orleans heat.

Back then, when people in New Orleans spoke of "the Coast," they were not talking about the Louisiana or Texas coasts, but the Mississippi Coast. Hotels sprang up in both Waveland and Bay St. Louis, with the Bay having as many as a dozen at one time and it was thought to be quite the thing to say you had your holiday on the Coast.

The old hotels are long gone and, unfortunately, so is the efficient train service. Several of my neighbors commute daily to New Orleans, taking about the same time commuting in their cars as the train once did, one hour, but now a rushed McDonald egg and biscuit and a plastic cup of coffee replaces the relaxed comfort of the club car breakfast.

However the main attraction is still here: the clean air and the pleasant sea breezes that spring up at around 10:00 a.m. each day.

Actually, it is the humidity rather than the heat that is the worst of the summer discomfort. The winds usually have a southern component and these come ashore heavy with moisture.

During much of the summer the temperatures at night are fairly reasonable. But as the temperatures drop, the air is unable to hold as much moisture and the humidity increases. As a result, we must still run the air conditioning in the evening and during the night, even though the outside temperature may be in the seventies.

To escape the heat, we have discovered a natural breezeway beside the porch at the east corner of the house. Here we've laid a low wooden deck. On this, Stella has slung a hammock between two of the large live oaks and I have positioned a chaise lounge and a table for drinks and dishes of Stella's summer ices or sorbets.

If there is a good breeze blowing, we can spend even the warmest days here making sure the trees don't get away, or the grass doesn't grow too loud.

Days are nice, but evenings are better. We often sit there in the cooler hours of the evenings, watching the bright white light of the day turn into the crimson colors of evening and then dark shades of the night. There are many ways we can spend our time, but there on the small deck I think we spend them the best.

***

Fall is one of the nicest times of the year on the Coast.

The heat of the summer eases up and some of the flowering plants that have been lying dormant in the heat start to bloom in abundance again. The water's still warm in the Sound, and for a while longer, I can go out wading with Jennie. Stella can still go wade fishing.

But things start to change.

They change slowly, but they do change. The drop in temperature means that the air can hold less moisture and we start to have light fogs in the late night and early morning hours. These offer scenes far different than what we see during the summer.

When early morning fogs occur, I sit and drink coffee and look out over a silent closed world lit by the diffused low-angle morning light.

I would sit at the table in the dining room – it's too damp to sit on the porch – my view limited by the morning fog to a few hundred yards of the beach.

To my right, Carrere's long wooden pier is almost a ghost. To my left, the ruin of Jeffrey's pier, backlit through the mist by the rising sun, is better defined, but still the definition is muted. If I look at the pier with binoculars, I see it as if it were a surrealistic etching of lines and soft colors.

At these times, the water at the beach edge is absolutely still, a silver-gray mirror reflecting the light back into the misted air above it. Each droplet of water in the mist re-reflects the light to other droplets and the effect of all these millions on millions of droplets reflecting and re-reflecting is a magical softness of light.

I remember during one morning's fog, a white egret slipping across my misted view, its reflection a soft shadow in the water, a noiseless movement in the closed scene.

I know that in an hour, the heating sun will cause all this to be gone, but for the time till then, I can sit and watch a world of diffused light, of silhouettes, of muted shapes and still water.

Days in fall keep getting shorter as the year progresses. With the sun shifting farther southward in its daily arc through the sky, there is a little bit more slant to the light, the evenings last longer, and we have prettier sunsets.

We start to see new birds and yellow butterflies as the fall migrations start. Once again we hear the geese and listen for their honking call at night. They often stop for a day or so, resting from their journey in one of the two nearby ponds.

A few hummingbirds, really just one or two, start to hang around and we realize they will probably stay the winter. We now have a responsibility to clean and keep full some of the feeders we have outside.

The fall full moon is fantastic, seeming to hang forever low in the sky over the water. The night sky is clearer, you can see more stars and they appear more brilliant. The air is different, cleaner, with different smells. The cooler air produces a crispness about the new odors. When Jennie comes in from outside, she brings imbedded in her fur the distinct sharp smell of the earth and the new season.

It's a time of transition and it will pass. But until it does, we enjoy it.

***

WINTER can be sneaky.

Just when we're sure it won't happen for a while longer, wham, one of the weather forecasts is right, and we have a night in which the temperature stays below freezing for four or five hours. We wake to see frost on our neighbor's roofs and on the pickup's windshield. We see it also on the outdoor flowers and plants. The frost disappears as the sun hits the roofs and truck, but all of our outside flowers are gone.

The planting areas now have a bleak, wintry look despite the day temperature reaching into the fifties and sixties. Hopefully, the night before, we will have brought in those plants that can be moved. If we did, then we will enjoy their flowers in the inside gardens for the rest of the winter.

Oak fires in the family room fireplace are now an everyday event and with it being cold, we spend more and more of our time either in the kitchen or in the family room in front of the fireplace's cozy heat. We light off the front fireplace only on weekends when it is cold or cloudy during the day. But in the evening, we go back to the family room.

During the Christmas holidays, both fireplaces burn continuously and their bricks start to radiate a warm heat into the rooms even from a low fire. Since the living room fireplace essentially divides that room from the dining room, both rooms now get the benefit of the warm bricks. The masons who made the two fireplaces evidently did good work and both fireplaces draw well.

For a while we used to get our firewood from the driftwood that washed up on the beach after a storm, but the beach crews have become too efficient and now we order wood from a professional supplier in the Bay and it gets delivered not as romantically, but more efficiently by truck.

Christmases are normally fairly mild. The large photograph in our family room shows a Christmas day years ago when a large winter high had pushed the water out into the Sound and the daytime temperature hovered in the low 70 degrees. The last few years have been exceptionally mild as well.

New Year's goes by quickly. To celebrate, we often have a neighborhood party at the house and there are large bonfires and noise and lights from the fireworks lit off on the beach and we all kiss and hug at midnight and we wake up in the morning and it's a new year!

Our winters vary in intensity, never the same from one year to the next. Every five or so years we actually have a snowfall. The dogs go outside and chase the falling snowflakes and seem surprised when they catch one and there is nothing there.

If we have an early snow before a real hard frost, the snow may well land on the outside flowers still blooming. When this happens, we have this odd scene of snow on the ground with impatiens and vincas sticking through the snow under a slate gray winter sky.

On some days we have a winter fog. We wake to find the world about us shrouded in a fog unlike the gauze-like pastel fog we'd seen in fall. Our surroundings are now encased in a cold, damp, depressing gray light. These conditions stay sometimes for several days, with perhaps, if we are lucky, a brief break at noon, then a return to the fog in the afternoon.

At night, when I look out at this fog I expect to hear a foghorn or bell. I have memories of sleeping in the bow of a ship on Newfoundland's Grand Bank and waking to hear the foghorn from the ship's bridge.

It was a mournful sound, blaring out in a cadence of once every two or three minutes. Lying there then, listening to the horn, the gurgle of water moving by the steel hull next to my bunk, I did not realize I would not hear these sounds again except in my head in a place in winter on the shores of the Gulf of Mexico.

***

Spring comes in spurts. It leaves you not sure if it's real or not. Can you plan on it; can you start your garden? Put the tomato plants in too early and there is a late frost and you have to start again.

Stella's philosophy is simple. Go ahead and put the plants in early. If a late frost hits them, all you've lost are a few plants. But, if a frost doesn't hit them, you have tomatoes a couple weeks early. Since I don't have much to do with the planting and yet get to eat the tomatoes, I think it's a good philosophy.

But then comes a moment when you realize that spring is really here and that the cold is really gone. And with the spring, the rains start. I don't mean the gentle spring rains of the "April showers bring May flowers" variety; I mean the heavy, one-, two-, maybe three-inches in an hour variety of rain.

The panoramic views you get of the storms from our beach house are startling. You can sit on the porch and watch them come, usually moving down the coast from the west, from New Orleans. You know they have just been pounded and now you're going to get it.

The sky is dark blue at the horizon, now lightning, distant thunder, a show of power, subdued at first, but then growling louder and louder, Wham! Wham! Wham! Closer and closer, maybe wrapping around to the back of the house and whamming with an impressive light and sound show just north of us.

And then Stella coming home and saying people are drowning in the shopping center one mile away and "can you believe that the rain stopped completely at the railway tracks just a little way up the street!" Around us, the roads are dry.

Or in front of the house, you see moving far across the water, majestic horizontal lines of dark blue power, heavy squall lines, moving with feathery curtains of rain below the clouds, and always lightning and the bass, ever present, thunder, while you sit in sunlight watching the show.

Or closer in, almost on top of you, and the lightning and thunder are almost continuous, non-stopping, on and on and on and on.

Or it comes sweeping across the water directly at us, black and menacing with crackling lightning, thunder and wind, rolling across the water and land, curtains of opaque rain, sheets of it hitting the water, making a line of flattened water to mark the advancing, hard rain.

Then it is here, and you are chased into the house by the large, cold drops of rain that are hurled under the porch roof by strong gusts of wind.

Then there is a steady fall of rain, receding rolls of thunder, and we know it is through with us and moving on to pay a visit to the people in Long Beach, Gulfport, Biloxi, Ocean Springs, and won't be back till tomorrow afternoon.

***

Sometimes on a spring night I'm awakened by a soft muzzle touching my arm.

It's Jennie, our Weimaraner. I lie for a second and listen. Soon I hear it, a soft roll of thunder to the west. Jennie is soul-terrified of thunder.

Of all the dogs we've had, she is the only one that has been allowed to stay in the house at night -- a relic of her accident when I had to tend to her through the long night. She'd picked up chasing trucks and caught one. Afterward she became accustomed to being inside.

She's usually very good, sleeping under the desk in my office. But now she's in our bedroom and she is terrified.

She sits there looking at me, her head a dark shape in the dark of the room. I lay still, stalling, not wanting to get up. Then I hear again the muted sound of more thunder in the distance, but now a little closer.

Jennie's dark head turns to each side nervously. She nudges me again, almost impatiently, with her damp nose. Both she and I know the thunder is crawling in the night sky down the beach toward us.

I also know that if I don't get up, she will try to get in bed with us. Accompanying that knowledge is the fact that she weighs almost eighty pounds and she is scared.

I force myself to get up, sit for a moment on the bed's edge, and then rising, start walking groggily to the back of the house. Jennie follows closely behind me.

It's the weekend and Stella and I are sleeping in the front bedroom. It's spring and rather cool and it's a long walk around the house, through the dining room and into the kitchen. Behind me I hear Jennie, hers claws clicking faintly on the ceramic tile floor.

Through the kitchen window you can see lightning flash in the west beyond Bayou Caddy. For some reason, the thunder seems to be much nearer and every time it sounds its approach, Jennie moves closer so she can touch me as we walk. She knows it's not the lighting but the thunder that can get her.

Now we stop for a moment; she sits, nervously resting one of her front paws on my bare foot. She sits looking intently to our west, her paw never moving away from its "accidental" position. I offer to put her outside on the side porch; there is an immense crash of thunder, she declines.

We continue our walk farther and farther back through the house, past the pantry, past the hall of storage closets and bookshelves. Then we are at the door to the garage. When she realizes where we are, she balks. She knows what's coming.

I open the door and order her into the garage. She sits back on her haunches firmly. She won't go. I finally manage to push her out and quickly close the door behind her.

Through the small glass window in the upper part of the door, I see her go to the two plastic barrels near the door that the other dogs we had had used as doghouses. The barrels are snug and provided a privacy for the dogs that they liked.

She crawls into the nearest one. Then there is a particularly loud crash of thunder almost overhead, and she comes quickly out, looking toward where I stand at the door.

I snap my head back from the window and listen. There is quiet, then there is a scrape and rubbing sound. I know by this that she has gone back into the barrel. I relax.

I think now she will stay in there till the storm has passed. I stand and listen for a moment to make sure. It remains quiet. As I stand there, I hear around me a broad engulfing sound, a growing patter. The rain has come to join the thunder. There is now a lot of lightning.

I start walking back through the house. As I pass through the kitchen, the noise of the rain hitting the house changes to a roar. It hammers on the atrium plate glass as if from a giant hose. The noise of the rain is everywhere around me and every so often there is the louder crash of thunder.

This will be a two-incher, I'm sure. I continue retracing my way. The rain is all around me, the noise of it and the thunder seems almost continuous. The lightning lights my way through the rooms of the house.

Once in the bedroom, I get back in bed. I realize that I'm chilled and quickly pull the warm covers about me.

Stella stirs, "Where did you go?"

"It was Jennie, she heard the thunder."

"Oh."

I lie there and listen.

There is still thunder, but now it's become muted as it moves away to our east, toward Biloxi.

The rain has slowed and now has a persistent steady beat. This rain will go on for a while and its sound is becoming a patter that is almost soothing. I let the noise help me relax, to ease my way back to sleep.

I say something to Stella about the rain and the early spring plantings we had put out in front the day before. But she's asleep.

I listen to the rain for a little while longer and then I join her.

THE ONE PENNY CHIP

...Perhaps there is a game-piece sorter within us that marks with superior wisdom what is truly important in our everyday existence and what is not. We all seem to have that sorter. ...

Last night just as the sun was setting, the sky, the beach, the house, all were suddenly bathed in a rich rose hue. Everything and everywhere the color touched was transformed into something different, something magical, something that had not been there moments before.

Then, in just a few moments, it was all gone. Twilight became night and the few moments of rose red light were gone from my view as if they had never been.

This is the joy of living on the beach and watching it and the water beyond. It is a show with a variety of times and spatial scales.

Sometimes you become entranced by an egret dancing in the tidal shallows. Its apparently drunken dance is actually designed to scare up small fauna burrowed in the mud of the receding tide. But whatever the reason, it's comical to watch.

Sometimes it's a flight of pelicans fishing a color line in the water just a few hundred yards out from the beach. Sometimes it's the silhouette of barges and shrimpers or low storm clouds on the horizon.

Sometimes all of these can be found collectively in a single scene, sometimes in parts of many scenes spread over days. Sometimes whatever it is, takes only a few brief moments to see and then is gone. Sometimes it all blends together; becoming the background vistas of a long, lazy summer afternoon that seems to last forever.

The broad view of sky and water and beach is always there, and the passage of time constantly renews this view with grand, fresh variations. Wait a moment, a day, a month, then look again and there will be a different something to see.

I have a photograph of my daughter walking up the beach from Carrere's pier. Looming behind her is the great dark mass of a summer thunderstorm moving in from the west. In the photograph, Cathy is a small object overwhelmed by the overall menacing grandeur of the approaching storm, the broad waters of the Sound, and the long stretch of bright sand.

The whole scene is a study of blue and gray contrasting with white and yellow, and the small object which is Cathy giving it an added vibrancy. I really don't need the photograph; I can remember it in my mind's eye which is softer and in many ways better.

All of these views, these scenes, whether morning, evening, summer, fall – sit in my mind like little color chips for me to call up when needed, to look at, to turn over, to rub with my mind's memory till they glisten in the soft light of thought.

"I remember, I remember" is a game that old people play, but it is good to be able to play the game at any age.

Even now, when I walk along the beach and either stare down at the foamy, tea-colored water washed by a wave at my feet, or watch a gull slipping along a layer of air over the water, I feel I'm building up my chips, my game-pieces for the time when I can do nothing else but play the game.

We all do that as we move along from day-to-day; build up our game chips. But truthfully, the game-pieces don't collect the way we think they should.

We see something we think is important and try to freeze that something in our mind to remember later. We tell ourselves that what we are seeing, doing, feeling, is important, that we have to remember a first kiss, a graduation, a new job. Later, long later, we find that what we tried so hard to remember is not there, it's all vague and replaced by things that at the time didn't seem important.

Perhaps there is a game-piece sorter within us that marks with superior wisdom what is truly important in our everyday existence and what is not. We all seem to have that sorter. I remember vividly something from when I was very young that seemed as nothing then.

I was at a candy counter. An old woman sat on a stool behind the counter. I remember that her hair was mostly gray and tied in a bun. She had on a blue loose-fitting dress and wore no make up as old people did then and her eyes were bright with a cataract in one.

But at the time, my mind was not set on her but on deciding which of the candy on the counter to buy. "How much is that?" I pointed to some chocolate candies in a tray. The woman got up from the stool and looked over the candy counter at me and then down to where I pointed. "Three for a penny." My fingers moved slowly to where some mints lay heaped in a cardboard box.

"They're a penny apiece," said the old woman.

She watched me for a moment longer then returned to her seat and continued her looking out a window in the rear of the store. I remember it being spring and that the back yard she looked out on was filled with damp dirt and had a wooden fence around it.

I looked at the candies some more and then made up my mind. "I'll take one of them." The old woman turned and looked at me as if seeing me for the first time.

I pushed the penny toward her across the glass top of the counter and she rose slowly and looked down to where I pointed. A cardboard box in the glass case held long limp whips of licorice.

She slid open the case and took out a single black whip. She gave it to me, took my penny and, dropping it into a cigar box, closed the case and sat back down to renew her staring at some old memories in the view of the rear window.

Without looking back at the other candy or the woman, I walked out into the bright street and I went toward the curbing. In the gutter, a small stream, a residue of a recent rain, floated a cigarette wrapper to the distant corner.

I began walking carefully along the curb's jutting edge; a slip now became a thousand-foot fall into the river raging below me. I bit my lip in concentration and watched as I carefully placed my feet along the thin stone, the licorice waving from one of my outstretched arms.

I didn't think anymore of the old woman -- only of the blue-gray granite curbing, of my balanced, swaying body, and the sun sweet smell of the spring air.

This was long ago, but I can still smell that tangy air and see the blue-gray granite.

Like my daughter walking on the beach, like the sunset last night, that view, that chip will always be with me.

HOLLY AND THE SNAKES

...Black as Holly is, he is almost invisible from where he crouches high on the limb of the tree... We have taken his picture on several occasions under different lighting conditions, and unless he opens his eyes, all we can see in the developed picture is a black blob; no real definition of anything recognizable. ...

We now have a cat.

Before all of you who have cats start looking for something else to read, let me say that this is our first cat. Stella and I are not cat people and till now have shared little love for cats. But now we have one.

We got the cat because of the snakes. But I'll get to that in a moment.

It's a male, it's black, and it's eight months old. We call him Holly. It's an awkward name that I find difficult to call out from the porch when we want him to come inside. To see what I mean, go out on your porch and yell "Holly" real fast four or five times.

I think for his age he's a little heavy. Stella says he's not. To prove this I weighed him by holding him and standing on the bathroom scales. Or I should say, trying to hold him. What with his wiggling and all, 6 or maybe 8 pounds is extremely close to what he weighs.

Knowing his weight is important since he has picked up vaulting as a sort of a major sport. Vaulting it seems is something he can do and vaulting is something he does.

I like to lie on a lounge on the low deck beside our porch. The breezes are perfect there, and on a hot afternoon I lie in the cool shade and breeze, relax and forget about the things that I am "supposed to be doing."

About a foot away from the lounge is a low branch of a live oak that stretches across the deck about three feet off the ground. Stella's hammock is close by and the oak is one of the two live oaks that hold up her hammock.

She's normally in it doing the same thing as me – talking, reading, and watching the sky and the beach. Usually after about two or so pages of my book, I close my eyes to "rest them."

It is when I am in this completely defenseless position that Holly's vaulting starts.

He gives no warning. Just a swift hard jab as his 6, or maybe 8, pounds lands in the middle of my perfectly relaxed stomach, then as the air is pushed out, his rear feet push down hard, very hard, and the 6, or maybe 8, pound mass vaults from my stomach to the tree limb. In seconds, he has run far up on the limb and has turned to watch what effect his world-class double vault has had on my relaxed peace of mind.

Well, I am up and I'm yelling.

Stella stares at me from her hammock and tells me to calm down. Since we've had Holly, she has turned into that worst of all fanatics, the newly converted cat lover. To her, Holly can do no wrong and she won't listen to anyone telling her otherwise.

So of course when I point out to her what the cat had done, I get no sympathy.

"Move your lounge," she instructs me. "You know he will do that if you keep it there. Your lying there just attracts him. Move somewhere else. Move over there."

She points to a place on the deck in the hot sun.

"Why should I move?" I answer and, giving up on getting any consideration, glare up at the cat.

Black as Holly is, he is almost invisible from where he crouches high up on the limb of the tree staring with his green eyes back down at me.

We have taken his picture on several occasions under different lighting conditions, and unless he opens his eyes, all we can see in the developed picture is a black blob, no real definition of anything recognizable.

Finally, Holly turns indifferently about on the tree limb and climbs farther up into the tree's large interior. He's soon gone from sight.

I look up after him for a few moments; then satisfied he is indeed gone, I return to the lounge and resume reading. Within a split second, Wham! Wham! I get hit again.

Sitting up, I see racing across the porch the disappearing unmistakable back end of a black cat.

***

Inside the house, Holly likes to do his vaulting using as an exercise horse the back of Jennie, our 75-pound Weimaraner.

Holly will leap from ambush at the unsuspecting dog, vault onto her back, dash along her spine toward her head and then rather spectacularly leap off as Jennie's head whips around and her teeth snap at empty air.

All in all, the two get along together fairly well. When I go back to my office in the rear of the house, the two follow me. Holly often dances ahead, crouches in ambush behind some obstruction and then as we go by, stands on his hind legs and bats at Jennie with his paws.

Jennie allows a little of this, then finally pushes Holly over, holds his squirming body down by the shear weight of her head and nuzzles him roughly in the stomach.

Once in the office they settle down and I often find Holly sleeping with his head on one of my feet and Jennie sleeping with her head on the other.

However, Holly normally prefers to spend most of his time sleeping somewhere on my desk, usually as close as he can get to my computer. He is usually well behaved and, after a bit, I forget he is there.

Yesterday, I found he had squirmed himself as close as he could to where I was working and had fallen dead asleep with his nose just lightly touching the keyboard.

***

Like I said, we got Holly initially because of the snakes.

We had started to see them around the outside of the house about a year ago. One bit Jennie in the cheek and her head swelled up to half again its normal size.

Then a workman killed one in the garage. "Pshaw, it's just one of them pigmy rattlers," he said. "It'll take bites from two of them kind a snakes to kill ya."

Well, gee!

But mostly we've found them near the porch. Among the numerous wives' tales I was told to do to get rid of them, spread lime, mothballs, etc, the simplest seemed to me was to get a cat.

Several people told me this. They would listen to my snake problem and then nod knowingly and say, "Get yourself a cat."

Well, I did, and now we have Holly. Since then, we have seen only one snake, so maybe there are fewer snakes than before.

I'm not sure though. It seems that most of the time I see Holly he is not out "snaking" like I think he should be, but rather stretched out in some awkward position, sound asleep on the porch.

I'm uneasy; I feel somehow, that there are snakes equally as relaxed, sleeping *under* the porch.

We're keeping Holly, he does sort of grow on you, but I do want to get rid of the snakes. I'm thinking of asking the people at the hardware store to drop off some lime.

THERE'S MISSISSIPPI RIVER MUD IN THE BAY OF ST. LOUIS

...The river water ... once it started to the east, it kept on going! It flowed past Bayou Caddy, past my house in Waveland, past the Bay of St. Louis, past Gulfport, and even reached as far east as Biloxi. There it finally turned south and began flowing out of the Sound through the passes in the offshore barrier islands, particularly Ship and Horn Islands. ...

For some reason, tourists to the Mississippi Gulf Coast seem to be confused on the geography of Mississippi.

They often seem completely surprised to find that the state of Mississippi has a seacoast on the Gulf of Mexico. When they do come and see the quiet waters of the Mississippi Sound, they are equally surprised to learn that the Sound is not connected in some way to the Mississippi River.

They seem to be disappointed by all this, almost as if we on the Coast are pulling some type of trick on them and hiding our river. They know we must have it here somewhere, – maybe in that marsh reserve near Pascagoula?

But we know better and to us, the Mississippi River seems a long way from where we live on the Gulf and the thought of any Mississippi River water washing up on our beaches seems to be less than a remote possibility.

Yet this is what happened several years ago. For several weeks, cold, muddy Mississippi River water flooded the width of the Mississippi Sound as far east as Biloxi. It intruded into the Bay of St. Louis and worst of all, washed up on the sandy beach in front of my house.

This is how it happened.

In March 1997, the U. S. Army Corps of Engineers, concerned by the rising waters of the Mississippi River at New Orleans, decided to relieve the high water problem by opening the locks to the Bonnet Carre Spillway located a few miles above the city.

This on the face of it seemed logical. The Corps built the Bonnet Carre Spillway for this purpose. The Spillway is an immense concrete structure stretching from the Mississippi river to Lake Pontchartrain with a large set of gates at the Mississippi River end. Having made this huge waterway, it would seem the logical way to relieve the problem of too much water in the Mississippi River would be to open the gates.

It turned out to be not that easy. There were several very strong pros and cons proposed by extremely vocal environmental groups as to what would happen to the ecology of Lake Pontchartrain as a result of introducing Mississippi River water into the basin of the lake.

The most important of these considerations was that the lake is brackish. As a result, the lake has its own ecosystem that depends on the water having a certain amount of salt. Introducing fresh water, yelled the con voices, would disturb the balance of that ecosystem.

Also, they pointed out, the Mississippi River water is much colder at this time of year than the lake water. And, it is rich in mineral fertilizers and contains trace metals that are not normally found in any abundance in the lake.

There were other items, but these few give the general idea of the opposition to releasing the river water into the lake.

Conversely, there were pro voices raised equally loud that presented very positive aspects to introducing the Mississippi water into the lake. Large quantities of fresh water would, they said, be actually beneficial. Even the mud carried by the river water was touted as having beneficial aspects.

Consequently, there was quite a to-do in the general New Orleans area when the Corps opened the spillway gates on March 17 and Mississippi River water flowed into the lake.

Openings these gates took several days and crowds gathered to watch the water pour out from the river onto the spillway and into the lake. They even had it on television. Whether you were for or against opening the gates, the opening was very impressive.

To us on the Coast, the entire noisy hullabaloo seemed to be just some more of the strange nonsense that takes place periodically in our neighboring state. It was of interest to us only in a very abstract sense and, when one really thought about it, was on a par with their trying to open a gambling casino in their downtown area or their trying to convict their governor of wrong doing.

To us, it didn't seem important if it did happen or didn't happen, but it was fun to read in the newspaper at breakfast or watch on the television news at night.

***

At the time, I was part of a group conducting a study on the "red tide," a poisonous algae bloom that had taken place for the first time the year before in the Mississippi Sound. This had been disastrous to our oyster industry, and we were trying to find out if it would repeat itself in the following year.

Whereas the events taking place in Louisiana were amusing, the effects of the red tide on the marine life as well as the seafood industry was not. Many of us were involved in trying to find out why we were suddenly being hit by this plague and to see if we could find a way to warn us in time if it did happened again.

As a secondary interest, we were studying how a fresh water toxic alga found in small amounts in the brackish waters of Lake Pontchartrain would react to the introduction of large amounts of fresh water.

My primary work in the study involved studying satellite imagery looking for signs of the red tide reoccurrence. To expand this to look at the fresh water algae bloom in the lake, I simply enlarged the area of the imagery I was processing to the west to include Lake Pontchartrain.

I was pleasantly surprised to find that the river water flowing out of the spillway into the lake was easily seen in the satellite visible imagery. It seems muddy water, at least Mississippi River muddy water, is highly reflective.

Each afternoon I would look at the day's imagery and watch the progress of the Mississippi River water as it moved through the lake.

Think of the lake as a somewhat flat oval with the Bonnet Carre Spillway at its southwestern corner. From this corner, river water flowed into the lake, bulged out a bit and then, entrained in the lake's counter-clockwise circulation, moved eastward along the bottom of the oval, the lake's southern border.

Lake Pontchartrain has a natural exit for overflow water at its southeastern corner. Actually it has two such exits there, Chef Menteur and the Rigolets, both of which empty into Lake Borgne.

Both passes are several miles long and comparatively narrow. As an indication of their continued use in bringing water into and out of the lake, the passes are quite deep, being fifty or so feet in places.

By April 6, I noted in the satellite images indications that the Mississippi River water was flowing through Chef Menteur and the Rigolets passes and emptying into Lake Borgne.

I had expected this, of course, and, in the days that followed, looked for the river water to flow eastward while hugging the Louisiana marsh coastline and then turn south and flow into Chandeleur Sound. All of this lies somewhat west of the Mississippi Sound.

As with many preconceived expectations, it didn't happen this way.

The river water did turn east as expected. But once it started to the east, it kept on going! It flowed past Bayou Caddy, past my house in Waveland, past the Bay of St. Louis, past Gulfport, and even reached as far as Biloxi. There, it finally turned south and began flowing out of the Sound through the passes in the offshore barrier islands, particularly Ship and Horn Islands.

Our group was astounded. While in the back of our minds we knew this could happen, to see it so graphically displayed in the satellite imagery took us aback.

To get a closer look at what the imagery was indicating to be taking place in the Sound, I hitched a ride on a Mississippi Department of Marine Resources plane and flew the entire length of the Sound. What I saw from the plane was every bit as startling as the satellite imagery indicated.

The muddy Mississippi River water flooded the entire width of the eastern Sound. I had the pilot drop low when we flew over where I lived and I could see the muddy water had discolored the water in front of our house. Moving on, I could see that propelled by the tide, some of it had moved into the entrance of the Bay of St. Louis.

In fact, muddy water was visible from the mainland clear across approximately ten miles of water to the barrier islands. It wasn't till we flew past Biloxi that we could find the eastern limit of the muddy water.

Look at the map on pages 4 and 5. Essentially the river water had filled all the area on page 4, with a strong element of the flow hugging the northern coast of the Mississippi Sound.

What we had in our naiveté, considered being a Louisiana problem was ours as well. And we were caught flatfooted, unprepared in any way to study the situation. The water was there and it was too late to send up a howl of protest.

***

After about 3 trillion gallons had flowed over the spillway, the Corps began the laborious process of reinstalling the gates. This took about a week. By late May- early June, the satellite imagery indicated that the last remnants of muddy water had passed through the Mississippi Sound and the barrier islands passes. Lake Ponchartrain quickly returned to the pre-deluge clarity and shortly thereafter the waters in the Mississippi Sound (including the waters in front of my house) also returned to their normal dark tea coloration.

Since then, no long-term harm to Lake Pontchartrain has been indicated by the studies that were conducted at the time, although some studies are continuing.

As to the Mississippi Sound, without a baseline of data to use for a comparison, no in depth study could be made. However, it appears that the Sound was not adversely affected for any long period by the Mississippi River water intrusion. Like any good estuary, the Sound seems to have shown its inherently healthy nature and flushed the material out through the barrier island passes.

***

But there was one thing that did occur that has ramifications we haven't really thought through as yet. It was a small event unassociated with the flood of muddy river water, yet given the breadth of the flood, suggests that we on the Coast had better keep a closer watch on what takes place in Lake Pontchartrain.

During the last days of the open spillway, a fire broke out in one of New Orleans' sanitation facilities. Until the utility was repaired, a large quantity of raw sewage poured uncontrolled into the southern portion of the Lake Pontchartrain, mixing with the passing Mississippi River water.

When this occurred, we looked in the imagery for some indication of this contamination. The sewage signal was too small and was lost in the overall Mississippi River water reflectance.

But we knew the sewage was there and it was just a matter of time before it went through the Chef Menteur and the Rigolets passes, turned east, entered the Mississippi Sound and flowed by the beach in front of my house and was introduced into the Bay of St. Louis.

As evidenced by its ability to flush out the muddy waters of the Mississippi River, it appears that we have a healthy, vigorous estuarine system. This is good.

But it takes time to flush itself out.

What we must remember is that as with many things in nature we have a tightly interwoven system, with no single element isolated from the others.

The history of what happened several years ago indicates that any spill of toxic material in far-off Lake Pontchartrain can affect us here on the Mississippi Gulf Coast.

Although it is true that the toxin may eventually be flushed out into the Gulf of Mexico, it can, in the time before that flushing is completed, drastically harm our local health or ecology.

We have to be watchful and very careful.

LISTER'S POND – PART 1

...In the pond... in front of me was a small island with a tall white egret sitting regally in a large tree, posed as if for a picture. Mullet were jumping in the pond around me, indicating the pond's tidal connection, and two turtles basked on a log projecting from the water. All around me were the muted noises of a wetland in full use. ...

Today was one of those beautifully crystal clear autumn days, the crisp air giving a hint of the cold that will come in a few weeks.

Displays put on by autumn days like this show the uniqueness of living on the Mississippi Gulf Coast. It makes you realize how very nice it is to live here.

I thought of this the other day when my wife, Stella, and I drove along Beach Boulevard in the Bay north of Highway 90. We had just turned north of the little triangle area at Second Street, and found ourselves gazing at a stretch of marsh that neither of us had noticed before.

It was the perfect time of both day and year to see it, the sun at the right angle and the clear air giving it a crisp look that in summer is often flattened by heat and moisture. The marsh lay spread before us, its grasses invigorated by recent rains and the cool weather.

The clean sweep of the bright yellow grass of the marsh butted against the dark trees along the shore. Flowing through it all were the dark brown waters of a small narrow bayou.

The bayou appeared as a meander from a break in the mass of marsh grass. Farther back, you could trace its course by the indentation in the broad sweep of grass. A brilliantly blue sky sharpened the scene, accenting rather than diminishing the broad spread of soft pastel colors.

We on the coast are lucky to have places such as this around us. We find them in sudden openings in the brush alongside the roads in Waveland, in the Bay, and over in the Pass.

And there are a lot of them.

Unfortunately, we normally go by these scenes too rapidly to properly digest their beauty. We hurry by scenes of soft, almost elusive beauty that we see only by chance encounters such as occurred to Stella and me that day.

Worse, we too often pay lip service to our often-repeated pledges to protect this beauty. Too often our attitude changes when that protection involves our own land. Land we want filled or bolstered for a dock or some such private use.

I found this happening to a tidal pond that faces the beach a short distance from my house last week. In one day, heavy equipment turned a beautiful wildlife habitat that I had admired for years into something that, when the grass lawn becomes established, would more resemble an English deer park than a Mississippi coastal pond.

I was deeply saddened by this. The pond has played a strong part in my realizing the delicate role that small tideland pools play in the ecology of my immediate beach community.

I discovered this pond twenty-two years ago when we first moved into our new beach house. The pond was half hidden behind some tall live oaks, in an area I wouldn't normally go. Gretal, the Weimaraner we had then, had strayed and I went looking for her. As I passed the large two-story brick house next to the pond, the owner came out and, pointing to the pond, told me where I would be able to find my dog.

Sure enough, Gretal was in there and I coaxed her out of the water, wet and muddy. Holding her by the collar, I looked around in wonder. Deep in the brush as I was, I could see much more of the pond than I could ordinarily see from the beach road.

In front of me was a small island with a tall white egret sitting regally in a large tree, posed as if for a picture. Mullet were jumping in the water around me, indicating the pond's tidal connection, and two turtles basked on a log projecting from the water. All around me were the muted noises of a wetland in full use.

When I came back out, I found John Lister, the owner of the brick house, waiting for me with a water hose. Together, we washed the mud off of Gretal and we talked. He told me the story of his house and the pond that Gretal had taken her bath in.

He said that in the very early 1800s, the pond and original house on the property is reputed to have been used as a storage area by a cohort of Jean Lafitte, the pirate. For years, this large sprawling wooden house was called the "Pirate House" by the locals.

Hurricane Camille in 1969 demolished any trace of the wooden structure, throwing much of the debris into the pond. Lister rebuilt a two-story house, using the bricks that formed the cellar storerooms of the original house. The bricks from the storerooms easily furnished the amount of bricks needed for the new house.

After clearing the pond of debris from Camille, Lister let it return to its natural state as a wildlife preserve. For want of a name, the locals referred to the pond as Lister's Pond. And in fairness to the memory of my friend, it will always be that to me.

As the years passed, I had to fetch Gretal many times from Lister's property, either from the pond or the area immediately behind it where Lister kept several Shetland ponies. I would go after Gretal and she would come back with me, running in large circles down to the pond's edge.

Mrs. Lister liked Gretal and would call her up to her kitchen and feed her Belgian chocolates. When I went to get Gretal, she would tell me of the ghost that lived in the new house.

From her second story window, I could see the pond in the long shadows of the late afternoon. To me the scene recalled the coastal marshes in which I had worked as a young man. Somehow, I thought it would always be as I saw it then.

I was wrong.

Mrs. Lister died and Lister remarried. As time passed both he and his new wife died and the heir broke the property into two parts, selling the house separately from a larger parcel of land that contained the pond.

A wealthy New Orleans family bought the land with the pond and, combining it with some adjacent property, began to build an extensive weekend compound.

Early one morning in late October, large trucks carrying earth-moving equipment parked on the compound grounds. Within the hour, to the surprise of the Waveland city council, and neighbors (including myself), the destruction of the habitat began.

In investigating what had occurred to allow this, I was told that the New Orleans owners had approached the Corps of Engineers with the offer to swap a parcel of wetland in Pascagoula for the wetland rights to Lister's Pond. The Corps agreed.

The land clearing and paper work done and gone, we locals were faced with a *fait accompli*. There was, I was told, nothing that could be done. The New Orleans owners had apparently crossed all the right "T's" and dotted all the right "I's".

I went over to look at the scene yesterday.

Lister's Pond, as I knew it, is gone. The small island is cleared of all brush and is completely exposed. The protective seclusion that much of the wildlife find necessary to breed is gone.

There is little left of the protective shoreline brush and marsh grass that bordered the pond. Soon, the local ecological fauna that depended on this small marsh/pond will find the area is no longer viable and die out. And, since the pond will no longer function as a breeding place of essential fauna, our local fishing will be affected.

Slowly, but surely, the amount of wetlands in Waveland, in Bay St. Louis, and in Pass Christian are diminishing. Soon, they will diminish to the point where it can no longer maintain our region's rich fauna as we know it today.

When these resources disappear, the unique wonder of what we see all around us today will go with it.

And with this disappearance another part of the life we know and love will be absent from the view our children and children's children will have in future years.

Perhaps that marsh area Stella and I found so movingly beautiful near Second Street will be gone next year.

If not next year, perhaps the year after that.

LISTER'S POND - PART 2

...Gretal would bark and dance about looking at the water flowing out of the culvert and then suddenly dip her muzzle in the water and take large, gulping bites out of the water. Then, dancing about with her short tail whipping about in a frenzy, she would look in the outflow for more of whatever she was eating. ...

There is an inherent dynamic wonder to living in a house bordering a beach on the Mississippi Sound.

From the very first days we began living here, Stella and I have been struck by the ever changing vistas in front of us; vistas that at times lulled us to complete relaxation by their seemingly endless serenity or startled us by their shows of violent beauty.

But always there is in all of these scenes an ever-present vigor, a throb of vitality, of rich life.

There is one startling example that I will always remember.

One morning in early fall, shortly after we moved into our house, I noticed what seemed to be rough water far out in front of us on the Mississippi Sound.

From our porch, the "rough" water stretched for miles along the horizon in both directions. It looked strange to me, not right somehow. I called to Stella to come outside and to bring with her a pair of binoculars.

By the time she came out with the glasses, the "rough' water began to change its shape. Great sections of it seemed to rise, as if it were smoke, slowly flowing to form long, low, swirling streamers in the air that in places would sink to retouch the water and then would rise again in undulating waves.

I held the glasses up to look closer. The streamers were ducks, thousands on thousands of ducks! They were rising and sinking in long dark swarms across the entire horizon of the Sound.

We watched, entranced, not believing what we were seeing. The magnitude of the amount of ducks that were involved was beyond our comprehension.

All too soon, perhaps in less than a half-hour, the birds were gone and the horizon was still again. That was twenty-five years ago, but I remember the scene in all its startling aspects as if it had happened yesterday.

We never again saw a migration on the scale of that fall day, but we have seen other migrations, some quite large, of ducks and other birds, and quickly learned to expect and savor the brief time these travelers spend with us.

We have learned to listen in the fall for the distinctive call of Canada Geese. Sometimes these large birds will stay for a day in one of the two nearby ponds. Their call in the evening will have us running outside to see them flying high in the red gold sky of the dying day.

We all have these vivid memories of natural events that have occurred in our lifetime. They make up both the substance and the value of living in coastal Mississippi.

Lately, however, I have wondered about the ducks we saw on that magical day and the fact that we have never seen anything on that scale again. Perhaps the skyway they followed has changed or there may be many other quite natural reasons.

But the fact remains that we have not seen that large a migration again.

I wonder what marvelous sights of either large or small natural events were common here fifty years before us? A hundred years? What natural events that we no longer see were common occurrences in our grandparents' time? Events that years ago gave them the same pleasure, the same feeling of awe, that the duck migration gave us, but that no longer occur?

I wonder what natural events that form the present ambiance of our coastal life won't be here for our grandchildren to see?

Will they hear the Canada Geese? Or see them in the night sky?

Will they see the pelicans fishing or the herons wade in the shallows?

And if they no longer occur, how much has our presence contributed to their disappearance?

***

Several years ago, we had a Weimaraner named Gretal that loved to roam the beach in front of our house. On several occasions I noticed that she would spend time splashing in the outflow running out of the wooden culvert emptying Lister's Pond, the pond a few hundred yards west of us. This is the same pond that the wild geese and ducks loved so much.

Gretal would bark and dance about looking at the water flowing out of the culvert and then suddenly dip her muzzle deep in the flowing water and take large, gulping bites. Then, dancing about with her short tail whipping in a frenzy, she would look in the outflow for more of whatever she was eating.

It took awhile before I found out what it was she was feeding on; I had to look close, very close.

Finally I found it.

It, actually they, were small fingerlings, the baby larvae of fish that, having reached a certain age, were emptying out of the pond to continue their growth in the open waters of the Mississippi Sound.

Gretal would hover about the shallow water of the culvert's entrance during an outgoing tide and when a large group of the fingerlings would appear in the outflow, she would slurp them up in noisy, joyful gulps.

Gretal's snacks were not even an inch long. They had hatched from roe that fish had deposited in the marsh grasses that rimmed the edges of Lister's Pond. There they had grown, protected from most predators by the tall grasses. Upon maturing, they poured by the thousands through the culvert into the open waters of the Sound, there to be the feed of larger fish, birds and, on occasion, Gretal.

Some of the fingerlings, some very few, would escape the fate of being food to the many and grow into mature fish. These mature fish would in turn return to Lister's Pond to deposit more roe. And so the cycle would go on as it has for hundreds on hundreds of years.

These fingerlings are a major element in the food chain that makes up the ecological stock in the immediate waters in front of our house.

The key word here is "immediate."

Think of the culvert as a source of these essential feeds. As you go farther and farther from this source, the amount of food decreases and, if the immediate regional life must continue in equal abundance, there has to be another food source. Not necessarily a large source, something about the magnitude of Lister's Pond.

And so there is. About three hundred yards to our east is another pond, the second of the two ponds I spoke about earlier. There, minute young fish would pour out as they mature and add to the immediate area's general food stock or replenish the region's fish.

All along the coast there are these small, but extremely vital, pockets of wetlands, each contributing its measure to the abundance of the regional fauna.

But Lister's Pond is no longer what it was.

The marsh grasses so essential to the protection of the fish larvae are gone. All that is left is a sterile tidal pond with smoothly graded sides laid out in a manicured park of grass and various plantings for the out-of-state owners to come on weekends to enjoy. It ahs become a park that one might find in Illinois, New York, or, in fact, just about any place in the continental U. S.

It's former unique beauty as a rich Mississippi tidal pond has been totally destroyed.

A few years earlier, the pond to our east was similarly terra-planned and its productivity drastically curtailed. As a result, the waters in front of our house depend on other small regional wetlands for both food and fish and the area is not as rich in fauna as it was in past years.

Gretal has been gone for several years and I miss her antics and her joyful dance in the waters of the culvert.

But then if she were here, she would be disappointed. I think this spring there will be very little coming out of Lister's Pond for her to eat.

THE NIGHT WOLFDOG FOUND HIS HOME

...Laura says that from her position on the ground, she saw a dark mass hurl itself viciously at the man, noisily trying to reach his throat. She said the only thing the mass didn't have was a cape and background music. ...

His name wasn't "Wolfdog" to begin with.

When Stella and I first saw him, he was just another of the strays left by the summer visitors to wander the roads. He came up to the porch from the beach road and sat in front of the sliding glass door looking in. Stella and I were just inside having breakfast.

He sat patiently watching us as we ate. Stella, a pushover for strays, went out finally and gave him something to eat.

As he ate, however, even she could see that beyond that faux timid air was a more self-assured dog, a dog that was looking for a permanent home. We quickly agreed that our house was not going to be it. We fed him and made him move on, which he did good naturedly, going on to check the other house on our side street.

Over the next few days, he became a neighborhood fixture, appearing at back doors of the various houses and giving his "I'm just a poor homeless waif, etc, etc.", act with little luck beyond table scraps.

When he tried his spiel at Barbara and Laura's place, however, he hit pay dirt.

In fact, he had captured Laura's heart but not Barbara's. "No more animals," said Barbara and that was the way things stood. At least that was the way Barbara thought they stood; Wolfdog had a different opinion and picked a comfortable bush on the side of the house and waited.

***

A couple of weeks later, Stella and I were just getting in bed when we heard a loud crash coming from the side street beside our bedroom window. Quickly lifting the blinds, we saw a car had crashed into a utility pole across the street from our house. The pole was toppled half over and a woman was trying to get out on the passenger side of the car.

Stella quickly picked up the phone and called the police. I hurriedly put some clothes on and went out to see if I could help. When I got to the car the woman was already out. When I offered to help her, she pushed me aside, announced she was going "back to the party," and headed up the street.

I looked inside to where the driver was slumped over the seat. The smell of alcohol filled the inside of the car as well as the sound of loud snores. The driver was fast asleep! There appeared to be no blood or indication of serious injury and I backed out, prudently deciding to wait for the emergency vehicles.

By now Stella had joined me as well as several neighbors and we all began talking at once, pointing at the downed utility pole, the car beneath it, and the woman weaving her way up the street. Then we heard yells coming from the direction of the party.

The exact events are best told by Barbara or Laura. I will try to tell as best as I can, what they told me later.

The party at the Dill's, across from Barbara and Laura, had been in full swing when the two had gone to bed. They were wakened sometime later by a loud crash from the front of their house.

Looking out the window they saw that a car coming out of the Dill's driveway had backed up on their front lawn and hit something. With a loud squeal of tires and a revving of the engine, the car began driving away.

Barbara and Laura, both still in their bedclothes, went running out to see what had happened.

They could see the car going erratically down the street, just missing several parked vehicles, and then smashing into something that brought it to a stop. Somewhere near the front of their lawn, they could hear a rushing noise as if air was escaping – the car had hit the gas meter and gas was hissing out of the ruptured line.

"Don't worry lady," Laura heard a voice yell out. "I'll take care of that."

She looked across the street and saw one of the guests from the party was coming over to where they stood. He was obviously drunk. In his right hand, he held a wrench. In his left hand, he held a cigar. It appeared to her to be lit.

She immediately started to yell at him to stay away, but he grabbed the damaged meter and told her in a loud voice that everything was going to be all right. He would fix it.

She grabbed him trying to pull him away from the wrecked meter and the escaping gas. He yelled at her to get out of the way and when she wouldn't, he shoved her roughly to one side, throwing her on the ground.

Then out of the bushes, slobbering and snarling horribly, came Wolfdog!!!

Laura says that from her position on the ground, she saw a dark mass hurl itself viciously at the man, noisily trying to reach his throat. She said the only thing the dark mass didn't have was a cape and background music.

The man dropped his wrench and raised his arms to protect himself. But it was no use. Wolfdog was at his moment of destiny and he knew it. He kept coming. In desperation and yelling at the top of his lungs, the man raced back across the street to the Dill's house, Wolfdog hard on his heels.

***

To us in the neighborhood, the aftermath looked like the end of the old Marlon Brando movie, "The Wild One." Police cars, tow trucks, utility company vehicles, ambulances were everywhere cluttering the street.

The neighbors stood on their lawns in the dark. The glow of the various rotating yellow and red lights illuminated the little groups of faces on each lawn.

Finally, the last of the vehicles drove away and we each went back into our respective homes. Tired from all the excitement, Stella and I went back into ours and went back to bed.

Up the street Barbara and Laura went in through the front door of their home and Wolfdog, their new dog, went with them.

A TIME TO BE CAREFUL AND A TIME TO BE WISE

... "You know," he said after a moment. "You have had some unhappy things happen to you and you have blamed them all on this car. You are an intelligent man. You know that this is just a car. It does not breathe. It is not alive. It cannot think." ...

This Friday won't be the thirteenth. I know, I've checked. I don't want you to think I'm superstitious; I'm not.

In fact we have a black cat that is so black that, if he closes his eyes in a dim room, he disappears. He runs in front of me, literally "crossing my path," all the time and it doesn't bother me. I did try kicking him when he did this at first, but he's too fast and thought I was playing some new game and started to do it all the time. So, I gave up.

But it doesn't hurt to stay on the safe side of things.

I had an old Chevy many years ago that impressed this on me. Let me tell you about it.

To be blunt, the car hated me. I got it by default as part of a settlement. It was my only means of transportation and I was stuck with it and, unfortunately, the Chevy seemed to feel it was equally stuck with me. It sometimes showed its displeasure in big ways. For example, letting the hood fly up as I was going down the highway. It was only after a passing Samaritan helped me get it back down and secure it with wire that I was able to drive on.

But more frequently, its dislike appeared in little ways, losing the gas cap so that the gas evaporated and I ran out of gas on a lonely country road. Or the oil cap came off and when I opened the hood I discovered an engine coated with oil. Or… well you get the idea, nothing seriously threatening to the car, but actions that provoked bad words from me.

The end of all these came one late evening when I was headed for an appointment that I absolutely had to keep. The car died and rolled quietly to a stop on the side of a little-used road. The water hose had burst.

I walked and walked and found a gas station. When I called AAA, they said it would be an hour before anyone could come. It was an hour and a half and then I had to endure a long tow to a garage that was still open.

The mechanic was Lebanese. He looked under the hood and shook his head. "You should take care of your car," he scolded. "If you look at the engine once in a while, you would have seen it needed a new hose. Look. See? The engine has oil all over it. It should be cleaned." I explained about the lost oil cap and said that the hose was perfectly good when I filled it with gas a couple of days ago.

He grunted and rolled under the car and tried to disconnect the old output hose from the radiator. It wouldn't come off and, in prying it loose, he slipped and banged his hand on the engine. A moment later, as he rolled out to get a new hose, he cut his other hand on the car's bumper.

Watching this, I felt I had an appreciative as well as captive audience. I proceeded to tell him about the one-sided hate relationship the car had been having with me.

"I've never done anything to it." I said. "I'd be foolish. I keep it clean. I wax it. I have it checked regularly. But it keeps doing things. Why just last week …" And I told him about the last escapade of the car's wrath.

He listened to me in silence as he took some hose from a rack and cut it, using the old hose as a gage. Rolling back under the car, he continued listening, as he struggled to get the new hose to go on. After a few moments, he rolled out again. He had cut the hose too short.

After carefully cutting another piece, he rolled back under the car again. I felt a certain tension in the air and stopped talking. It became very quiet.

Finally, with great difficulty, he got the new hose on and, rolling out, he wiped his hands on a rag, blotting carefully around the cut on one hand and the bruise on the other. After warily looking over the various engine connections, he got in the car and started it.

We both stood in silence, watching it idle. It seemed to be running very well.

"You know," he said after a moment. "You have had some unhappy things happen to you and you have blamed them all on this car. You are an intelligent man. You know that this is just a car. It does not breathe. It is not alive. It cannot think."

He leaned over the running engine and gestured expressively. "This is a machine. A piece of metal and rubber."

With that he disdainfully slapped the input hose, the upper of the car's two radiator hoses. This hose parted immediately and sprayed him with hot water. He jumped away from the car and stared at it.

"Are you burnt?" I asked anxiously.

He shook his head, turned off the engine, and went to the rack of new hoses. "This will take a few minutes," he said. "Why don't you go in the waiting room and I will call you when I am done."

I went inside and a little while later he came in with a bill to give to the cashier and said he would bring the car around to the front. I paid the bill, noting that he had only charged me for the first hose repair.

When I went outside, the car engine was running and he was standing holding the door open for me to get in. When I did, he leaned in the open window.

"You know," he said, "you must be careful some times. My mother in the old country when I left gave me some buttons. You know, regular buttons like the buttons you have on your shirt. She said if I have a problem to put one of the buttons beside the problem and the problem will go away"

He looked forward to where the engine was running. "I still have all the buttons. It was silly, you know, superstition. I don't believe. But I keep the buttons to remember her and maybe just in case..."

He backed away and spread his hands expressively, the palms up. "Try it. Put a button in the glove compartment. It won't hurt. Maybe it will help. What do you have to lose?"

I nodded, thanked him and, engaging the gears, drove away. Looking through the rear view mirror, I could see him watching the car as I drove off.

***

I didn't try the buttons.

I decided to go for stronger medicine. I made a few phone calls and a few days later I drove the car into a large lot filled with cars. I went inside the building, signed some papers, walked out a door on the other side of the building, climbed into a brand new 1969 baby blue Volkswagen beetle, and drove away.

They gave me twenty-five dollars trade-in on the old Chevy.

THE MISSISSIPPI SOUND AND THE BARRIER ISLANDS

... There are five islands in the 70-mile barrier chain. From east to west, these are: Dauphin Island, Petit Bois Island, Horn Island, Ship Island, and Cat Island. These islands are sand bodies with interior dunes that reach 20 to almost 50 feet in height. They are remnants of a barrier chain of islands more than 3,000 years old and have been worked and reworked by storms many times...

"I see two people in the one boat," yelled Stella over the noise of the plane's engine. "They're both fishing."

As I wrote the amount of people down, the pilot climbed back up to our one thousand foot cruising altitude and headed the small plane eastward along the coast of Cat Island.

In moments, we spotted some more pleasure craft in the water and, making a tight banking turn, we again dropped down for a closer look. This time the boats were on my side of the aircraft and I had to squirm about in my seat, pushing against the pull of the turning aircraft, to count the people that were fishing from the several boats.

We were temporarily taking part in a bi-weekly aerial survey around the barrier islands, the loose line of islands along the southern side of the Mississippi Sound. These unpopulated, relatively untouched islands act as both a natural playground for us Coastians to enjoy and as a physical barrier that protects our coastal communities from the sometimes-violent Gulf storms.

It was the playground aspect of the island chain that was paying for the aircraft and allowing Stella and I to be out here.

We were taking part in a state-sponsored count of people engaged in sport fishing from and about the islands. There were other counters simultaneously taking part in the survey with us. These were in boats and on the local docks checking to see what kind of fish were being caught, how many and where. The survey was part of a two-year research project being conducted by Mississippi State University Research Center for the Mississippi Department of Marine Resources.

Although I am not an ardent fisherman, Stella is. I knew she was staring enviously at the people we were counting in the boats.

We on the coast are lucky to have this broad expanse of water and islands available for this pastime, especially so easily assessable from our homes. I say "pastime," but I know Stella's attitude toward fishing and I suppose a stronger word might be appropriate.

That others share her enthusiasm is evidenced by the numerous boats parked in driveways and backyards along the streets and back roads of all of our local coastal communities. Each of these appears ready at short notice to "go get us some fish". From our plane, it appeared that many of these boats were out here today.

From the front porch of my house on a clear day, I can see one of the barrier islands, Cat Island, the island we were flying over at that moment.

However, the view of Cat Island from our aircraft height was markedly different from the flat, distant view from my porch. As the plane banked to continue its run to the east, I could see the entire length and breadth of the island, its interior dunes and small ponds. It was a splendid view.

A strong haze was present and I couldn't see Ship Island, the next island in the chain. However, below us we could see in clear details, the long linear rows of trees along the dunes and the equally long black, quiet ponds in the interior that ran parallel to the dunes.

Along the shore of the island, I could see beneath the surface of the water, the whirls and convoluted contours of the shallow bottom. Basking in these shallows toward the island's northern tip, were several porpoises.

I pointed these out to Stella and the pilot hearing me, obligingly dropped down to allow us a closer look. They appeared to be Bluenoses and the leisurely fluid movement of their bodies against the curved yellow, light tan lines of the shallow bottom produced a strong study in contrasts. We circled watching them for a few moments and then proceeded to the next island to continue our fishing census.

Although it was a pleasant way to spend a morning, my real reason for volunteering for the flight was to view the other aspect of the barrier islands, that is, their ability to protect the southern coast of Mississippi from the ravages of Gulf storms. In this instance, I was particularly interested in looking at the damage caused by a storm that had occurred during the winter.

Our flight took place in June of 1998. Earlier, in February, we had had one of the worst winter storms to hit the area in a number of years. I had been hearing that the shores of several of the barrier islands had been altered by the storm. Now, almost five months later, as we continued our flight over Ship and Horn Island, I was seeing those changes.

I was surprised just how extensive the changes were. The eastern end and Gulf side of each of the islands showed the most changes to the shoreline. Here large amounts of the beach and interior ground had been washed away. Even after months since the storm, I could see stands of slash pines and even a few scattered live oaks toppled into the water or uprooted and lying in the island shallows.

I always have to mentally kick myself when I see such scenes. Normally in our everyday life in a suburban area or arboreal parks, fallen trees and damaged limbs are quickly cleared and the place is made neat and clear of clutter. When a limb falls down from one of our trees about our house, I'm on top of it in seconds to clear it away.

Here in the natural settings, no one does such things and the storm debris are there for months till they rot or in the case of the trees such as these in the water, get carried away by the coastal currents. What I was looking at was a normal, actually healthful, natural process, but it takes a little adjustment in one's thinking to see it objectively.

As we flew over the western ends of the islands just the opposite of these scenes was evident. Here, new sand accretion had enlarged broad areas of the beaches and sand extensions projected out into the passes and north away from the Gulf into the Sound.

It appeared that, although the eastern ends and southern sides of the islands had undergone severe erosion by the storm, the western ends had been extended.

***

We have a tendency of thinking that the things we see around us in nature are permanent, that they won't change; or if they do change, the change will be gradual. This is really not true. The forms of the land we see are not permanent; they do change and those changes can often be quite dramatic and sudden.

When I went to school, the prevailing thought was that grand changes in the earths landscape take time. My geomorphology courses preached the idea that the earth's landscape evolved gradually, with many of the landform changes taking centuries to occur. Evidences that this was not necessarily true were all about us, but the thinking of the times was blinded by this faulted central theorem.

Fortunately, these views have since swung the other way and the belief now is that, while gradual changes do occur, catastrophic changes of both small and grand scale are equally responsible for the shape of the land.

In the case of the barrier islands, I was seeing that both slow and catastrophic changes play strong roles in forming the islands sizes and shapes.

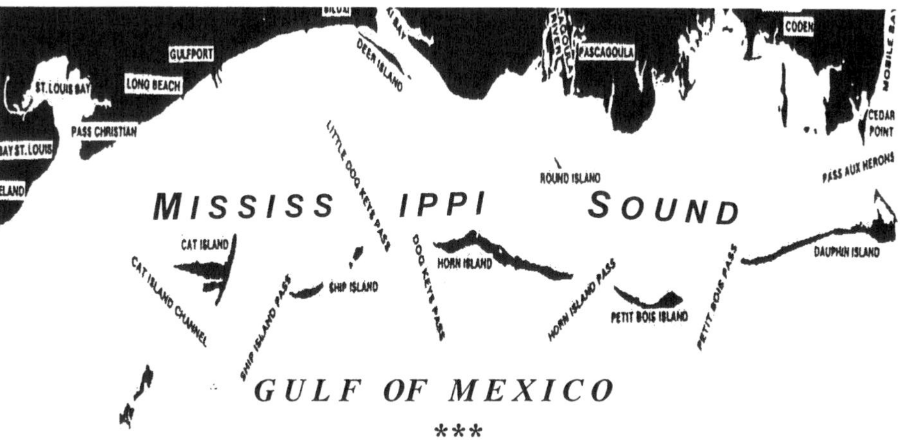

***

There are five islands in the 70-mile linear barrier chain. From east to west, these are: Dauphin Island, Petit Bois Island, Horn Island, Ship Island, and Cat Island. These islands are sand bodies with interior dunes that reach 20 to almost 50 feet in height.

The two mechanisms for much of their present formation have been both storms and a general westward setting current. The storms acting viciously to make the large obvious changes, left scars that remain for long periods afterward. The slower but almost continuous action of the westward setting littoral currents, day after day picking up the sand grain by grain and moving it from the east to the west added and subtracted from their shapes (the source area of the moving sand lay to the east toward Florida).

The present islands are remnants of a barrier chain of islands more than 3,000 years old and have been formed and reformed many times in that period. About 1,500 years ago, when the Mississippi River delta moved to where it is today, the islands' replacement sand supply was drastically decreased and the islands changed in size and shape.

Cat Island, the island I can see from my house and the first we flew over that day, is the oddest shaped of the island chain. It looks like a well-gnawed T-bone, a partial result of present day processes and its earlier history. Since it is protected by the Mississippi River Delta, the western portion has retained its shape from the earlier period.

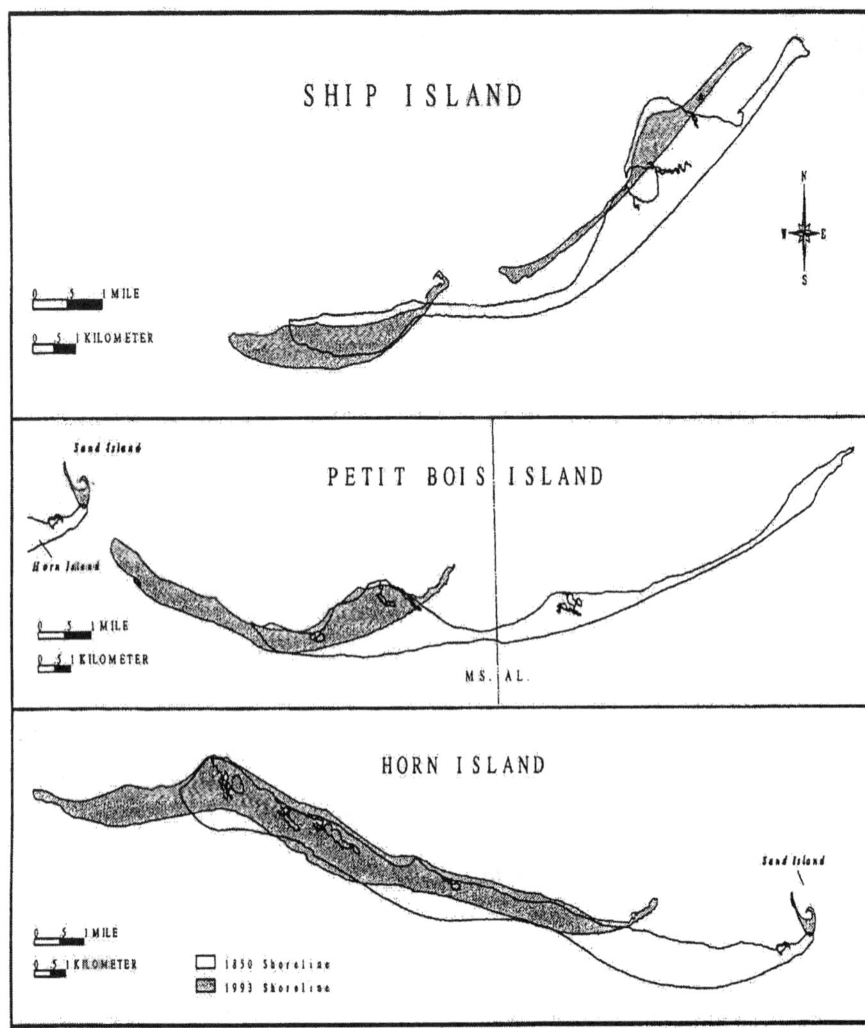

At this time, the islands appear to be somewhat stabilized to their present size, nourished by sand from sources to their east. Although some changes have taken place in the last two or three centuries, these changes have been relatively minor. The above drawings show the changes between the 1850's and 1993 (taken from a paper by Otivos in *Marine Resources and History of the Mississippi Gulf Coast Volume 2*, published by the Mississippi Department of Marine Resources).

If the Mississippi Sound did not lie behind the islands, the islands would probably form one long unbroken sand barrier. But the Sound is there and as the coastal tributaries drain into it, the accumulating water exerts a pressure to get out past the islands and empty into the Gulf. The passes between the islands form the means to relieve these pressures.

There are a number of sources of such excess water: river runoff, storm surges and tidal action. The most prominent of these is the tides.

Normally, you would not think of the Mississippi Sound as a major tidal body since its diurnal tidal range in height is less than two feet. However, the Sound has an area of approximately 1,850 square miles. Even at just a foot or two, this is a lot of water and a large volume of water daily moves through the island passes.

Depending upon the phase of the lunar tide, the tidal currents generated by this volume of water result in strong currents (more than two knots) moving in the channels cut in the passes.

The pressure of the winds can cause an increase or hinder the tidal flow, depending on the wind direction and strength. In fact, meteorological events, such as the passage of cold fronts or storms can easily double the strength of the tidal currents.

We on the coast are used to seeing the broad tidal flats along the coast formed by the winds of a cold front pushing the water far out from shore. At these times the water rushing out through the passes can be quite strong.

As a result of this tidal action, four shallow passes separate the five barrier islands. From east to west, these are: Petit Bois Pass, Horn Island Pass, Dog Keys Pass, and Ship Island Pass. The water depth in the passes is generally less than 15 feet, except in the narrower tidal channels lying within the passes.

In these passes, the strongest periods of tidal currents have cut deeper channels and each pass has one or two such tidal channels. Presently, the maximum depths in these channels range from 46 feet in Horn Island Pass to 23 feet in Petit Bois Island Pass.

Like a well-balanced machine, the tidal currents keep these channels clean and clear, in perfect need for their flow requirements.

In fact it appears that the four passes are optimally situated and sized just enough to allow the present amounts of excess water to leave the Sound. When the surges from hurricanes exceed the normal amount of water, new passes are often cut in the islands. However, when conditions have returned to normal in the post-hurricane period, these new cuts gradually fill in.

The most recent cut formed during Hurricane Camille in 1969, the one splitting Ship Island in two, is very shallow and no permanent tidal channel has been formed. If the present trend of pass formation continues, this cut will probably be gradually filled and the two parts of the island merged in the next decade or so.

Now, for the interesting part.

These tidal passes and their deeper incised channels, along with the barrier islands themselves, are migrating westward due to littoral drift processes exacerbated by the occasional storm.

What we had seen as we flew over the islands were examples of that westward movement as well as the major forces creating that movement. What we had witnessed indicated that the island's movements take place during both short periods of rapid change and during less dramatic long periods of recovery and sand movement.

These abrupt and long-term actions result in the general westward movements of the passes and islands that is evidenced by the constant need to dredge the ship channels and the recent near loss of Fort Massachusetts.

Fort Massachusetts at the time of construction just prior to the Civil War was located equidistant between the Gulf and Sound shorelines and about 1,000 feet from the western tip of Ship Island. It is now approximately one mile from the western tip and is on the island's northern shore. If not for the efforts of the National Park Service in constructing a protective sand berm, the Fort would now be a brick island sitting awash in the Mississippi Sound.

***

Several weeks after that flight over the islands, I walked with Jennie, my dog, on the beach in front of our house. It was right after a heavy rain and the beach was partially flooded by water that was still trying to run off into the Sound.

The storm had built a temporary sand berm on the beach just at the water's edge. The water that had accumulated on the beach had to get by this berm in order to reach the Sound. It did this by forcing cuts in the berm.

As we walked, I watched the water draining through several of these cuts. Looking several hundred yards to my west, I could see that similar cuts had been made with almost mathematical precision in the berm all the way to the wooden culvert draining Lister's Pond.

What I was looking at in miniature scale was a stylized model of the Mississippi Sound, the barrier islands and the tidal passes! When I looked closely at the "passes", sure enough, I saw narrow, deep cuts, – the scaled-down equivalent of the barrier islands tidal channels.

BLUEBERRY PEACHES, STRAWBERRY JAM

...Beside the large shed where the farmer counts up your buckets is a small tree loaded with Mississippi peaches. The farmer doesn't like to sell the peaches: "There aren't enough for me to sell and for me and my wife to have some, too" But he usually gives me a basket free and I go home loaded with fresh blueberries and a little bit of heaven. ...

When I was a young boy in the Navy stationed in Newport, Rhode Island, I went for a while with a girl from Fall River, Massachusetts. She wasn't a very pretty girl, but she was pleasant, fun to be with, and when she let me kiss her, her kisses were a pure and wondrous delight.

To me Mississippi peaches are a lot like that.

If you put Mississippi peaches up beside the peaches produced by our neighboring states, they don't look as good. They're small, they don't travel easily, there isn't as much fruit to each peach; but once you take a bite … Wow! They have a wonderful pure peach flavor, they're sweet, they drip with juice …

I love the time in the spring of the year when they come into season and you can buy them from the road vendors.

That's the problem. There is no use going to the Save-A-Center or Jitney Jungle. These chain stores won't carry them because of their puny looks and short shelf life.

You have to look for them being sold by the side of the road and the vendors selling real Mississippi peaches are hard to find. Many try to sell you bad-looking Georgia or Alabama peaches and to be honest, a bad Georgia or Alabama peach is a bad peach.

Sometimes the season is bad and none can be had. I dream of going down a dark alley and some shady figure whispers to me, "Hey, mister. You wanna buy some Mississippi peaches?" and I wake up to find it was just a dream.

There is a place near Woolmarket where Stella takes me to on occasion to pick blueberries. I like blueberries with my waffles and in biscuits. They make good toppings for a whole bunch of things or by themselves, with just sugar and some heavy cream, they're delicious. So I say ok to please Stella and I go with her.

I'm really not too good at picking any kind of fruit and blueberries are no exception. Mostly I sample and look for bushes that have a lot of berries and find after a bit that my bucket is only half full and Stella has already picked two buckets. But it's nice out in the quiet of the country and I don't complain.

It's what happens afterward that I like.

Beside the large shed where the farmer weighs your buckets is a small tree loaded with Mississippi peaches. The farmer doesn't like to sell the peaches: "There aren't enough for me to sell and for me and my wife to have some, too" But he usually gives me a basket free and I go home loaded with fresh blueberries and a little bit of heaven.

Stella is good at making preserves and jams out of these seasonal fruits. Blueberries are good, but she goes hog wild with strawberries and these have to be "fresh", meaning we have to go pick them.

Now picking strawberries is not like picking blueberries. The berries don't seem to be as accessible and Stella can tell when I'm looking at a hawk or eating too many of my pickings.

But it gets done and that night she whips up some cream, treats the strawberries with sugar in a way to generate a little syrup with the berries and we have coffee and dessert out on the porch and watch the day end.

What strawberries that are left over, she preserves. Therein lies a bit of family lore.

One year Stella made a batch of strawberries that gave us about a dozen pint-sized jars of preserves. When she looked at them the next day, she was disgusted. She had evidently made some small error in her usual recipe. The preserves appeared runny and, while they had good color, they didn't seem right to her.

She was going to throw the whole batch out when I happened by and tasted them. !!!!! Unbelievable! I'm not a strawberry person. I'd rather put hot chocolate on Stella's homemade ice cream then use strawberries; but the preserves she had made from those particular strawberries were good!

For much of that summer, I put the preserves on about anything that laid flat on the table. Stella's pound cake and whipped cream were heavily involved in this and it was a wonderful summer. But, sooner than I thought could be possible, the jars of those fantastic strawberry preserves were all gone.

"I thought you made a dozen jars?" I asked.

"I did, but I gave some away," she said. "Now what's wrong? Where are you going?"

"I'm going out back to check! Maybe you gave away my pickup, too!"

"Don't be silly. I can make some more. Sit down. Quite sulking."

But she couldn't. And, as much as she tried in the years since, she hasn't been able to.

Thomas Wolfe said that you can't go home. Maybe he was referring to a greater mystery than a house in some distant town, maybe he was referring to my never being able to have any more of that wonderful batch of strawberry preserve, or maybe kisses from that long ago girl from Fall River.

But I do know this. Out toward Woolmarket there is a blueberry farm. And beside the large shed where they weigh your buckets, there is a peach tree. And if you go there at the right time of year and sit and talk a bit with the farmer, he'll let you have some of his peaches.

PIRATES IN THE MISSISSIPPI SOUND

... Lafitte and his Barratarians ... fought heroically in the battle, well deserving their pardons. Unfortunately, Lafitte was at heart a pirate and could not quit the life style he had followed for years. ... he moved his activities to Galveston Bay in Texas. Here, he was ... killed in a vicious sea action with a government sloop of war. ...

Pirates!

The word evokes an air of adventure! danger! mystery! Whether the actual thing was as romantic as depicted is debatable, but we have had our share of questionable adventurers.

Perhaps a little too much of them; the stories told about some of them are not nice. Captain Pitcher was one of the meaner ones to sail the Sound. In fact his men hated him so much that he didn't trust them and he built a place in a large tree so that he could sleep safely at night.

The story goes that this did not help as the men gathered one night and burnt both the tree and Captain Pitcher up in one good sized bonfire. His mean spirit is still supposed to be wandering around Pitcher Point in Pass Christian.

Then of course there are the Honey Island Swamp pirates, a group called the "Screech Owls." Led by Pierre Rameau, this was a group that terrorized the western part of the Mississippi Sound for a number of years and sold their loot in the long since gone logging town of Gainesville.

But my problem with all of these pirates is that their stories are all anecdotal, with little, if any, claim to being factual. They were here, that we know. Small amounts of their loot have actually been found and the stories of other buried treasures abound.

But what I would like to talk about here is one for which there is a great deal of factual information. This is about the most infamous of them all: Jean Lafitte.

In the very early 1800s, Lister's Pond and the original house associated with it were reputed to have been used as a storage area for pirate loot by a cohort of Jean Lafitte. The story I've been told is that a Mr. Donahue built a house by the pond in 1802, a time when the regional population was extremely sparse. It was a good time and place for such activities. And from all indications, it appears that something such as this was going on.

For years, the sprawling wooden house was called the "Pirate House" and postcards with its picture were sold in the local shops. Much later, the stories I've been told continue that bootleggers used the pond and the house as a staging area for smuggled liquor during prohibition. The liquor was supposed to have been brought in via an inlet where the wooden culvert now stands and placed in storage in the old brick warren of basements beneath the house.

Then came Hurricane Camille in 1969. Although the Waveland and Bay population has increased with the coming of the casinos in 1992, the pre-casino population still refers to events in their lives as "before Camille" or as "after Camille." The devastating physical and psychological destruction of the storm on the then small population provides ample reason for this. All the local beach houses were destroyed. This included the old Pirate House.

The storm demolished any trace of the wooden structure. John Lister, who had owned the original house, rebuilt on the site using the bricks that formed the cellar storerooms. This large two-story brick house still stands, although the pond has changed in character to a pretty manicured park and is no longer the beautiful tidal sanctuary for herons, egrets and other birds that Lister reclaimed.

Although as with the other pirates, there is a lot of anecdotal material about Lafitte's connection with the house or Lister's Pond, I've found it hard to get any factual information.

In my opinion, the pond and house were some type of smuggler's sanctuary and may well have been used by pirates. If it was, it was probably pirates from the Honey Island Swamp rather than cohorts of Lafitte. Indications are Lafitte wasn't even in this area of the world in 1802.

Lafitte's area of operations was Barrataria Bay, the large bay lying on the other side of the Mississippi Delta. Here, he was head of a rather large nest of cutthroats and their vessels. Although they operated under the flag of Carthagena, with some rather vague Letters of Marquee, the Barratarians were nothing more than common pirates and did little to disguise that fact.

On 2 September 1814, a British brig anchored off the coast of Barrataria and the brig captain, a Commander Nicholas Lockyer, approached Lafitte under a flag of truce. Commander Lockyer had with him letters from the fleet admiral, Admiral Cochrane, offering a large amount of money to Lafitte as well as a full pardon if he would join with the British against the American regional forces then being assembled in New Orleans under General Jackson.

Lafitte stalled in his answer to the British officer, while secretly sending a message to Governor Claiborne in New Orleans. In the letter he informed the governor of the British offer and stated that he would refuse the offer only if he and his group were given a full pardon by the United States government. Governor Claiborne and General Jackson countered the offer, stating that if Lafitte and his men joined in the defense of New Orleans, they would be given a full pardon by President Madison.

Lafitte acquiesced and the rest of this incident is written as part of the many stories associated with the Battle of New Orleans. Lafitte and his Barratarians, true to their word, manned several gun batteries at Chalmette and fought heroically in the battle, well deserving their pardons.

Unfortunately, Lafitte was at heart a pirate and could not quit the life style he had followed for years. After a series of setbacks, he moved his activities to Galveston Bay in Texas. Here, legend has it, he was finally brought to bay and killed in a vicious sea action with a government sloop of war.

***

So what has this to do with Hancock County and the Mississippi Sound?

Well, we had not seen the end of Commander Nicholas Lockyer, the captain of the British brig that unsuccessfully parleyed with Lafitte. He, rather than the pirate, Lafitte, figures prominently in both the Sound and County's history.

After his visit with Lafitte, we next see him and his small brig several months later forming part of the invasion force being assembled by Admiral Cochrane to attack and capture New Orleans. Admiral Cochrane boasted that he and his officers would be having Christmas diner in New Orleans.

On December 12, 1814, more than 10,000 British troops aboard an armada of 65 British naval vessels positioned off Ship and Cat Islands just outside the Mississippi Sound. The troops were going to their attack using barges, following a water route through the western Mississippi Sound.

They were not to proceed unchallenged. Seven small American naval vessels lay off the coast of Bay St. Louis and Waveland to watch the British movements. The small flotilla was under the command of a rather stubborn U. S. Naval Officer, Lt. Thomas Ap Catesby Jones (the "ap" in Lt. Jones's name is a derivative of the Welch prefix *map*, meaning "son"; hence Thomas, son of Catesby Jones).

Lt. Jones's command was a small one, all that General Andrew Jackson could spare to defend the entire coast. These consisted of five rather cumbersome gunboats, a small schooner *Alligator,* and the tender *Sea Horse*.

The British were well aware of the presence of the observing gunboats and the danger posed by their large guns. For this reason, Admiral Cochrane formed a volunteer unit of marines, sailors and soldiers and had them occupy a large part of the initial wave of invading barges. He put this elite cadre under the command of Commander Lockyer and gave him specific orders: destroy the gunboats.

Commander Lockyer assembled a fleet of fifty of the various launches and barges, armed them with forty-three cannon and loaded them with approximately a thousand of the volunteers. After an overnight rendezvous off Henderson Point, he set forth rowing toward the seven gunboats manned by one hundred, eighty-two Americans.

What followed was a running two-day battle fought first in the Bay of St. Louis and later just beyond Bayou Caddy. The men Commander Lockyer were fighting were not pirates but professionals in the fledgling U. S. Navy. They didn't back down, but stood and fought. The British were equally as stubborn and won the action, but not without a heavy price in casualties.

Commander Lockyer and Lt. Thomas Ap Catesby Jones were both badly wounded in the fighting. Commander Lockyer was given a hero's welcome back at the fleet and was later promoted to the rank of Post Captain for his role in the action.

Lt. Thomas Ap Catesby Jones, although the loser in the engagement, was also commended for his valor and rose steadily in rank until he made Commodore of the Pacific Squadron. His last action was the capture of Monterey in Spanish California.

Unfortunately for him, we were not at war with Mexico at the time and the War Department, in what I consider a rather spoilsport manner, made him give it back.

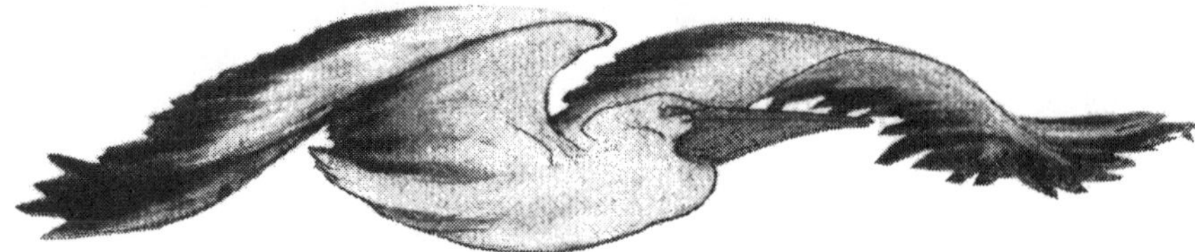

SUNRISE, SUNSET, MOONRISE AND THE GREEN FLASH

...But if you are blessed with a clear horizon, whether it is sunrise or sunset, at that moment that the sun rises or sets a wonderful thing happens, a momentary atmospheric blaze of brilliant green color called the green flash. ...

"What are we doing," Stella yelled at me. "It's too early to get up! It's cold! It's dark!"

This morning, I had wakened Stella before sunup and, wrapping a blanket around each of us, coaxed her to come out with me onto the front porch.

"You'll see, you'll see," I kept telling her.

It was no use explaining anything to her. On Sundays, unless she's wade fishing, she liked to sleep till about 8:00 or 8:30 and it was now 6:55. It was also cold, 43°, and the dew point was 32°. This low dew point indicated a very low humidity, an important factor in enabling us to see the phenomenon that I had gotten her up so early to view.

Jennie, wagging her tail in anticipation, came out with us, racing in broad excited circles on the lawn, in anticipation of what was obviously going to be an early morning adventure. When she saw that all we were going to do was settle in two of the lawn chairs, she lay down beside us with a disgusted grunt.

I directed Stella to look over the water to our east. Conditions were near ideal for what I wanted us to see; there were no clouds. On the horizon, the sun's eminent rising was indicated by a bright aura of light in the clear morning sky.

We were there to watch two things, the rising of the sun and, if luck were with us, an atmospheric sun-related phenomenon called the *green flash*. At 07:03, as prompt as one of Mussolini's trains, we saw the sun rise out of the water. It was every bit as spectacular as I expected. First, a little dot of bright, brilliant light that grew rapidly, almost explosively, a bright blob erupting up out of the water forming a big balloon of brilliant flame that grew and grew until the entire globe of the sun broke free of the water.

But no green flash.

Seeing the sun come out of the water is not as common as one might think. Normally, there is a morning haze, mist, or low cloudbank on the horizon that obstructs seeing it rise cleanly out of the water as we did today. Usually when we see first see the morning sun, it's already a few degrees in the sky emerging from this haze or cloudbank.

I had gotten up early and gone outside earlier in the week to try my luck on seeing the green flash. The humidity was also low on that day, but the early morning light revealed a faint mist on the horizon.

As the sun disc rose behind this veil, its color was a beautiful rose red that flooded everything with rich color and made the water luminous silver red. It was a lovely scene lasting only a few magical moments. While I didn't see the green flash, I was glad I had a chance to see this particular sunrise.

As an aside, watching the moon rise directly out of the waters of the Sound is an even rarer event. The nightly cooling of the atmosphere and the resulting dropout of moisture produces a haze that normally hides the rising moon at night as well as it does the rising sun at daybreak. But when you do see the moon rise out of the water, it too is a rather startling sight.

Its first appearance can easily be mistaken for an unusually bright star, then, as it grows out of the sea, it is obviously something larger than a star and much brighter. And then you stare amazed as you realize it's the moon.

I've heard stories of fire departments out west being called to go after a fire at some distant farm by callers fooled by the first sudden rich glow of the rising full moon. These may have been just tales, but the first time you see the moon suddenly emerge directly up from the water at the horizon you can easily see how such stories can have originated.

Sunsets offer another opportunity to see the green flash. However, our immediate coastline in Waveland and Bay St. Louis is oriented to look to the southeast and thus, when the sun sets to our west, it does so over land and the green flash can't be seen.

This is unfortunate since, from my experience, seeing the evening sun falling directly into the water happens more often than seeing the morning sunrise cleanly out of the water. I believe this is because in the evening the earth and air are still warm and the atmosphere can retain more moisture. Thus, the problem of low clouds or mist is less likely to occur.

But no matter, if you are blessed with a clear horizon, whether it is sunrise or sunset, at that moment that the sun rises or sets a wonderful thing happens, a momentary atmospheric blaze of brilliant green color called the green flash.

It is a rare phenomenon; things have to be just right. I have seen it only twice in a lifetime of going to sea. This – although as with this morning – I have stood and watched for the phenomenon many times.

In essence, the green flash is a fleeting spot of intense green light seen at the horizon immediately before sunrise or an instant after sunset. The effect is simply the passing of sunlight through the atmosphere, much as what happens when we see a rainbow.

Sunlight is made up of a collection of colors with each color having a different spectral energy. When sunlight passes through a raindrop, the spectral colors are each bent differently so that when they come out from the raindrop, they form the magnificent spread of colors we call a rainbow. The green flash is very much the same effect.

Each day at sunrise and sunset, sunlight passes through the thickest possible layer of our atmosphere and this bends the sunlight so that we can see it broken down into its spectral colors, just like a rainbow. Only in the case of the sun, this bending of sunlight results in colored arcs of light above and below the sun disk.

Just before sunrise (or after sunset) this forms a bright green glint of light just before the sun's edge rises above (or disappears below) the horizon. The flash itself lasts for about a blink of an eye, but is so brilliant, it dazzles the eye in that microsecond.

Because of various atmospheric conditions, the green flash is best seen in Hawaii. When I told Stella this, she said not to wake her up that early again till we were in Hawaii.

Well, perhaps I haven't seen the green flash as much as I would have liked to in my life. But I have seen some wonderful sunrises and sunsets.

I suppose that's not too bad.

ME AND THE SILVER RANGER

... "Howdy! Howdy! Ain't she a beauty? I can have you drive her home today, no problem. And I'll get you a good price on your Monte Carlo, too." I turned and looked at the salesman. He was almost a cartoon of a short, plump "good ol'boy. He smiled as if he was as happy as I was that we had found this truck. ...

"Paul, where is the bread?"

Everyone was glaring at me. I had been invited to join the Navy mailroom Christmas Party. Their Christmas Party food was always exceptional and I had worked hard to get them to invite me. But now I was both late for the party and had forgotten to bring the one thing they had asked me to bring: bread.

I looked around and spotted a number of loaves in a basket on one of the tables.

"But you have bread," I answered defensively.

"That was brought by Agnes who said that you would forget. Paul, if you don't bring at least one loaf of bread into this room, you don't get anything to eat." This was from Carol, the head of the mailroom and I could see she meant it.

Looking around the room, I could see similar commitments on the faces of the others in the room. I left, promising I would return with bread.

I was at the NASA test site and the nearest place to get bread was in Picayune, a small town about fifteen miles north of the site. I got in my Chevy Monte Carlo and started toward Picayune.

The Monte Carlo was a comfortable car, well broken in with two-hundred-fifty-thousand miles on the odometer (actually there were much more; the odometer cable had broken several months earlier). It had a large engine and I quickly covered the short distance to Picayune and got the loaf of bread.

However, just before picking up the bread, I passed the Picayune Ford dealership. There sitting in the lot, draped in large banners, was a silver 1989 Ford Ranger pickup with chrome wheels. It was a heady sight.

As I bought the bread, all I could think about was that brand new 1989 silver Ranger. For years and years I had been wanting a pickup truck and there sitting in that Ford car lot waiting for me was the pickup of my dreams. I wanted that truck!

I decided to be rational about it and not be too hasty. I would just stop and take a look at it and see if I could get them to come down on the price and then think about it for a couple days.

I left the bakery and drove slowly back to the dealership. I drove by twice. The truck was still there. Finally, I pulled into the car lot and parked near the silver Ranger. I realized that my heart was pounding.

Climbing out of the Monte Carlo, I began to look at the pickup more closely. It was a beautiful truck. In addition to the fancy chrome wheels, it had a black plastic bed liner, faux-wood dash and semi-bucket seats. The price was just a smidgen over $8,000.

"Howdy! Howdy! Ain't she a beauty? I can have you drive her home today, no problem. And I'll get you a good price on your Monte Carlo, too."

I turned and looked at the salesman. He was almost a cartoon of a short, plump "good ol'boy." He smiled as if he was as happy as I was that we had found this truck.

"I'll take it," I said before I could stop myself. "What do I have to do?"

About an hour later I was driving back to the NASA test site in my brand new pickup and joined the mailroom Christmas Party. I still had final papers to sign and needed my wife, Stella, to sign with me. She also worked at the test site.

At the party, everyone was happy and we sang carols, but I was the happiest of all. Or I would be if I could convince Stella what I wanted for Christmas.

Later, Stella looked at the pickup and said a few hard words. But I could tell that she too liked the truck. So, it wasn't too difficult to get her to go with me back to Picayune and together we signed the necessary papers.

Happy as a bee in a pot of honey, I then drove the pickup home to Waveland. (I found out later, they sold the Monte Carlo the next day.) Stella didn't say much, but I could tell she was pleased with it as well.

It wasn't till we got home that the trouble began. When Stella sat down and went over the papers she found that, while we both had signed for a twelve-month loan to pay for the pickup, the ownership papers were in my name!

She blew up! She grabbed the phone and called the dealership and preceded to tell them what they had done and what they were going to have to do about it. Her voice was raised and it was stringent.

I decided it would be best if I left the room, and as quietly as I could, I headed for the door.

One line I remember from the side of the phone conversation I could hear as I went out was, “What do you mean you didn’t think a lady would want to own a pickup truck!! Let me tell you…”

I wandered back to the driveway. There the silver Ranger sat there like it belonged, like it always should be where it was. I took the hose from the rack and washed off some mud that had gotten on one of the tires.

I walked around the pickup, looking closely to make sure everything was OK. It was. I wiped the windshield. There had been a spot.

The door to the house in the garage burst open. Stella came out storming, “They say it will cost another fifty dollars to change the title! I won’t pay it”

“You’re right, honey,” I said. “That’s a lot of money.”

She glared at me and then at the pickup and went inside, slamming the door behind her.

Stella got a car later, a Chrysler New Yorker. That’s all right. I still like my 1989 silver Ford Ranger pickup with its chrome wheels.

And best of all, it’s all mine.

... And Things That Go bump In The Night.[*]

...What I remembered most was my all-encompassing fear. No, not fear, terror! I had felt stark, unbridled terror! Terror of something I could not see. Something I knew was there with me in the dark. Something made up of the dark itself. Something that was always there, always a part of the dark, but only in my dream had been able to come out. ...

Let me tell you a ghost story.

The other night, I woke up terrified. My bedroom was dark except for a dim light coming through the doorway from the hall. I tried looking about me in the dark. Although I could not see anything, I could sense the strong reason for my terror.

There was something in the room!

I tried to get out of bed and found that I could barely move! I desperately tried to somehow get up! to get away! but it was no use.

I lay there exhausted by my efforts. Slowly, I realized that I was at the very edge of the bed. If I could only... Summing up all my strength, I pushed myself off the bed's edge and fell toward the floor. Using the momentum of the fall, I staggered upright and hurled myself at the doorway. Once there, I clicked on the light switch.

Nothing happened.

---

[*] Published on Halloween 1999 in the *Sea Coast Echo*

I was too terrified to turn around. Whatever was in the room now knew I was out of the bed and would now come after me. I knew if I could get the light on, it would go away. I flipped the switch repeatedly. Suddenly, it clicked, but instead of the room flooding in light, the dim light in the hall went out!

And whatever was in the room, was now right behind me.

I screamed, but all that came out was a low moan. I kept screaming, and screaming, and my moans became louder and louder. I felt a hand shaking me.

"Paul, what's wrong?" It was my wife, Stella. I had awakened her with my moaning. I was in bed, soaked in sweat. I could feel my heart pounding.

I looked around me at the familiar dark outlines of our bedroom. There was nothing there. Everything seemed perfectly normal. I said something about a dream to Stella, but she had already fallen back to sleep.

I closed my eyes and felt inward for whatever it was that had caused the terror of only moments before. It was gone; there was nothing, no trace of the terrible real presence that I had felt in my dream.

Sleep was out of the question. I got out of bed and, going into the bathroom, splashed water on my face. My heart had fallen back to its normal rhythm. Already the dream was fading from my memory. I had to strain to remember details that only moments before had been vivid reality.

What I remembered most was my all-encompassing fear. No, not fear, terror! What I had felt was stark, unbridled terror! Terror of something I could not see. Something I knew was there with me in the dark. Something made up of the dark itself. Something that was always there, always a part of the dark, but only in my dream had been able to come out.

Around me everything felt comfortable, the same comfort that epitomized and made warm the house that I had lived in for many years. I tried to feel once again what I had felt, but it was useless.

I was wrapped in a blanket of soothing familiarity that my terrifying dream presence could not penetrate. Around me the house cracked, a comforting noise, as if the house was shifting in its sleep. I headed back to the bed.

As I lay there, I realized that deep within all of us are goblins and ghosties. We carry on a very deep level phantasmagorias of terror; and, despite all the worldly cloak of daytime reality, they lie there waiting for some opportunity to rise up through our levels of consciousness.

They rise to the levels of our dreams or occasionally higher in our waking moments in dark places and at times when dimensions of reality are dim or warped.

But they are there, very real, lying deep down, permanently imbedded in our psyche, ghostly relics of some unknown primeval encounter. Somehow in my dream, I had released my demons, allowed them to emerge from their hidden pits.

I think we all do this at one time or another.

Think back. Do you remember having such dreams? Have you not caught yourself avoiding a dark attic or place? Placing the comfort of everyday reality between you and the unknown that stood just beyond your vision? You have, I know. We all have, every one of us.

And when we do, for a few fearful moments we become as one with the Cowardly Lion when he held tightly to his tail, closed his eyes and said,

"I do believe in Spooks,
I do believe in Spooks,
I do believe in Spooks..."

ONCE UPON AN OLD MATTRESS

... "That's to show you how to flip and turn your mattress so that it wears uniformly. See you flip it this way, then rotate it, then flip it again, then rotate, and you are back to where you started. If you do one turn every three months, then at the end of the year you have rotated it a full cycle." ...

Stella has decided that we need to buy a new mattress.

"What's wrong with the old mattress?" I asked. I didn't really get an answer; just that she doesn't like it, she has never really liked it, and besides it's old. Anyway, we need a new one.

I'll admit it's old. We bought the mattress, as well as a refrigerator, a washing machine, a dryer, a dishwasher and a garbage disposal all in one afternoon at Sears when we first built the house twenty-five years ago.

Except for our bedroom mattress, they're all gone now. Each one has long ago stopped running and was discarded. Which, I guess may mean something philosophically, but I'm not exactly sure what that something is.

When she first broached the idea of buying a new mattress, I went and checked the old one. It seemed in good shape. It's easily in as good a shape as the one that she likes so much in the front bedroom and that one is only fifteen years old.

We've started the "looking around" stage. We no longer buy things the same day we decide we need them; we "look around." This stage can sometimes take awhile. Our bedroom furniture took two years of "looking around," our living room furniture three. So now we are looking, but I don't think the mattress should start worrying about being replaced for a while.

When we went to one of the mattress places and began listening to the same pitch that I had heard several times before, I let my eyes wander to a small diagram set in the fabric at the base of one of the mattresses. It showed the mattress being flipped and rearranged in several proscribed positions.

"What's this about?" I asked.

"That's to show you how to flip and turn your mattress so that it wears uniformly. See you flip it this way, then rotate it, then flip it again, then rotate, and then you are back to where you started. If you do one turn every three months, then at the end of the year you have rotated it a full cycle."

I stared at him, not sure I heard him correctly.

"You turn the mattress how often?"

"We consider three months as the maximum time that people will go without turning their mattress. Of course, you probably do it more often. Just how often do you do it?"

Stella looked at me and then turned and busied herself looking at the fabric of a nearby mattress.

"Well," I said, "we had a thorough workover of the house for Pilgrimage in '91. I turned it then."

"No," said Stella. "That was in '92."

"Right," I said correcting myself. "It was in '92."

The salesman looked at us and then quickly proceeded to show us some of the advantages of the other mattresses. He never returned to the subject of flipping mattresses, but he did emphasize the ability of the mattresses he was showing to take heavy wear.

When we left the store and climbed in our car, I happened to glance up at the small windshield decal that stated the car was due for oil, lube and filter work.

I started the car and headed home, making a mental note to schedule the car for a trip to the garage and to tell them that it was time to also rotate the tires.

On the way home, we stopped at the Post Office. Among the bills and catalogues, I found I had a postcard from my dentist telling me that I was due for my six-month check up and cleaning. I made another mental note to call and make an appointment.

When we got home I took some sun tea from the refrigerator and told Stella I was going to sit on the lounge on the porch with Jennie. Jennie leaped up and down; maybe I would let her play fetch with the Frisbee. I didn't. Instead I relaxed and thought about the things that had been happening.

Somehow, I felt that things were getting away from me.

I was being told to see my doctor once a year, my optometrist and dentist twice a year, my car mechanic every 12,000 miles (for the car and again for the pickup), the vet once a year, have the air conditioner checked in the spring and the heater in the fall, the smoke alarm twice a year… The list goes on and on.

Now I'm being told I'm to rotate the mattresses every three months! The heck with it, I thought. Let someone else worry about flipping the damn mattress, I was going to worry about whether I should face to the right or to the left when I lay back on the lounge to take my nap.

Jennie took that moment to drop the Frisbee on my lap. I looked at her and a broad grin spread over her face as her tongue hung out. She pranced in anticipation and I threw the Frisbee.

She raced out and, leaping spectacularly in the air, caught it about four feet from the ground. It was a beautiful catch. I watched in appreciative wonder as she pranced proudly back with her prize.

Of all the things that had happened to me that day, I realized that she was showing to me the right perspective:

CARPE DIEM!

(Seize The Day!)

THE OYSTERMAN

... When the dredge comes in, the cold muddy water drips down on the deck and on the aprons of the men working. It chills the men's hands through their gloves as they sort the catch. There is a smell, a strong dank musty smell of the bottom over the catch and the spillover on the deck. ...

This morning's sky was a winter sky.

I felt cold looking out across the water to where the oyster boats were working the large reefs near Pass Marianne. The sky was a slate gray with the sunshine making a flat glare off the water. The boats stood out in this light as minute silhouettes, mostly small black sticks with squarish black bases.

During the October-through-June oyster season, a good many of these boats can be seen in several scattered clusters, dredging oysters from these large and extremely bountiful reefs, especially the ones over Square Handkerchief Shoal. They have been farming these reefs for more than a hundred years.

There had been a great deal of excitement out there a week ago. A tug pushing a string of two barges ran down one of the oyster boats. Two men had been on the boat. One of the men managed to grab a hold of a forward section of the lead barge and, scrambling aboard, saved himself. The other oysterman had fallen under and run over by the same barge.

Yesterday they found his body and today in the cold, I watch the boats back out there working the reefs.

Using my 60-power spotters scope, I tried bringing in details of the distant boats, but the moisture in the air at that distance made them swell to grotesque parodies of themselves. They remained bleak silhouettes, occasionally moving, but essentially black sticks growing out of bulging black bases.

Although cold for me watching from the comfort of my porch – it's in the low forties with a wind – it is undoubtedly even colder to the men working on the boats; the water temperature in the Sound is in the low fifties.

When the dredge comes in, the cold muddy water drips down on the deck and on the aprons of the men working. It chills the men's hands through their gloves as they sort the catch. There is a smell, a strong dank musty smell of the bottom over the catch and the spillover on the deck. Soon the dredge goes over the stern again and the boat swings about to make another pass at the oyster bed.

There are some oyster areas closer in toward the coast that are reserved for manual tonging, but manual tonging is slow work and these oyster areas are generally bare of boats. Almost all of the oystering here in the Sound is done using motor winches aboard motor-powered boats.

In the Chesapeake Bay where I lived years ago, the law read that the oysters had to be harvested by sail-powered boats. Because of this, the squat-sail, broad-beamed, wind-driven Chesapeake Bay oyster boats are as ambient a part of the Chesapeake water scene as the motor-driven boats I see out there on the Mississippi Sound today.

Because they use motors to move their boats doesn't mean that the work of the men harvesting the oysters in the Sound is not as hard as that of the Chesapeake men. It is. And it is cold and wet work, too.

However, there are many of us who like our oysters on the half-shell and/or in oyster stew and there is a good market for the catch. So again today the men are out dragging the beds as they have for a hundred or so years, pulling in the oysters from these rich reefs.

When I lived near Baltimore, we would often go out with friends on a winter afternoon and have oysters; oysters, which at the time I thought were harvested by oyster boats working in the Chesapeake Bay. They may have been, but I find that nowadays there is a good chance that the oysters served at a Baltimore oyster bar may well have come from oyster boats working the reefs of Square Handkerchief or Merrill Coquille Shoals in the Mississippi Sound.

A drive down North Street in Pass Christian will disclose proof of this. A number of large refrigerator trucks with Maryland and Virginia license plates are parked beside the several large seafood-shipping facilities. These trucks are waiting for oysters. When they are loaded, each truck will make a non-stop speed run to deliver fresh oysters to their northern city.

In the summer, Stella wade fishes in the water in front of our house. She would get up before daybreak and drive in the dark to Bayou Caddy to get live shrimp to use as bait. Just as I was getting out of bed at daybreak, she would be waist-deep in the water over by Carrere's pier, casting for trout for our lunch.

She would buy her shrimp at Bayou Caddy from the man who drowned when the barge ran the oyster boat down. He was a friendly person and would always kid her about how many fish she would catch that day and throw in a few extra shrimp "for luck."

She was upset by the news of the accident and, as they searched for his body, she asked me where they might find him in the Sound. I said, given the general circulation in the Sound, my guess was east of where the boat sank, the drift of the debris would tell them.

They've found him now and I'm sure the family feels closure.

Today, the oyster boats are out there working the reefs again and they will be every day till the season closes.

TRUTH AND CIRCUMSTANCE

...Then I heard a snuffling and the huge head of Lillie hung over my face. I was saved! I knew that I had to be badly hurt and there was no one home. But Lillie was here and Lillie would save me! ...

I've been brought up on dogs being the heroes of stories; *Lassie Come-Home* (the book, not the television series), *the Biscuit-Eater, Call of the Wild* ... the list is endless. All of these were stories of noble dogs loving and saving their masters from deadly peril.

As a result I came to believe that such perils constantly hover about us; that when danger threatens, it is the ever-watchful dog that will step in and, often at the risk of its own life, save us. And if there ever exists any doubt, one just had to look into the deep lustrous eyes of one's own stalwart canine and come away with the deep conviction that here is a dog that would go to any extreme to prove its love.

I believe I made it through childhood because I always had a dog. Tippy was a name a lot of them had, but I remember one with the distinctive name of Ralph. These dogs never left my side and then and now I'm sure that when I was very young, the presence by my bed at night of some long-ago Tippy kept *the-thing-that-lives-in-the-closet* from coming out and getting me.

We have always had a dog in the twenty-five years we've been living on the Mississippi Gulf Coast. Sometimes there has been just one dog, sometimes there has been more than one, in fact, for a number of years there were three.

These were all Weimaraners, noble-looking German pointers with brownish silver-gray coats and strange piercing hazel eyes. Weimaraners are fairly good-sized dogs commonly weighing eighty or so pounds.

Although they spent a great deal of time outdoors, they were basically housedogs. Once when someone asked Stella why we had so many large dogs in the house with us, she replied that it was because of all the closets. I could tell where she was going with her reply and stopped her before she could elaborate any further.

Actually, at bedtime, the dogs were put in the garage where they had some plastic barrels to sleep in. It was a comfortable arrangement and they seemed to enjoy it. The barrels were deep and on cold nights two would often double up in one barrel for warmth.

***

There are times in our lives when it seems that all the values we hold sacred are tested by a single event. This once happened to me and a Weimaraner we had called Lillie.

Lillie was a lovely dog. She had been the sole survivor of an ill-starred litter and I had nursed her by hand to ensure she lived. She was now big and strong and when she sat looking at me when I worked, it was obvious she knew what I was doing and would help if only I would give her the chance.

The time I am talking about involved my being on the roof covering the two fireplace chimneys for the coming warm weather – we have problems with nesting swifts.

The work went quickly and I returned to the ladder in the rear of the house over the garage and near the garden.

As I grabbed the edge of the ladder to descend, I looked down and saw Lillie patiently waiting for me. Just as I put my foot on the rung, the ladder started to slip away from the roof and in seconds I was dropped the nine feet to the ground.

What made it bad was that I was partially entangled in the ladder so that both it and I went down together. I landed on the ground on my feet, but the ladder was still tangled in my legs. It hit the back of my knee, twisting my leg and throwing me hard against the building.

I lay on my back, dazed, trying to catch my breath.

I started to mentally check various parts of my body for pain to see if anything was broken. This did little good; everything seemed to hurt. Moving even a little bit seemed to make every one of those things hurt even more.

Then I heard a snuffling and the huge head of Lillie hung over my face. I was saved! I knew that I had to be badly hurt and there was no one home. But Lillie was here and Lillie would save me! Lillie bent forward and licked my face.

"Go, Lillie. Get help."

She leaned forward and licked my face again.

"Go, Lillie! Go! Go! Get help!"

She looked down at me as if trying to decide whether she should lick me once more. Then her head disappeared and she was gone.

I had read and seen this a hundred times in books and movies. She would go to the neighbors and somehow tell them that I was hurt and they would come and I would be rescued! Everything was going to be all right.

I stopped trying to move and leaned back and relaxed. Things still hurt, but I knew everything would soon be taken care of. Although my chest hurt, I found that I could breathe without any problems. It was quiet. I started to relax.

Then I heard the noise.

I lay still and listened. I heard it again. It was coming from the garage. It took me a couple of seconds to realize what it was.

When I did, I became enraged and, rolling over, struggled to my feet. Everything seemed to hurt. My left ankle sent pain shooting through me. I grabbed a nearby garden rake and using it as a crutch and ignoring the pain coming from everywhere else, hobbled into the garage.

There was Lillie in her barrel – sound asleep! The noise I had heard was her snoring!

When she heard me coming, she looked up startled and, sensing trouble, retreated deep into the interior of the barrel. I stood in front of the barrel for several fruitless seconds, banging it with the rake and yelling, but she wouldn't come out.

Finally, I went to my Ford pickup and climbing in started the engine. I would get my own help!!

It wasn't easy.

My ankle was broken and the truck had a manual shift, but I got to the hospital where they put a cast on the broken ankle and pronounced that the rest of my hurts fell under the diagnosis of "assorted bruises." Bruises that hurt, but still just bruises.

I was assured that I would live.

It was harder driving home with the cast on, but I did and, ignoring Lillie in her barrel in the garage, went inside and waited for Stella to come home so I could tell her about my day.

When she came and I told her what happened, she said that if I hadn't been so mad, I wouldn't have been able to shift gears in the truck, so when you consider what happened, Lillie had saved me.

"Saved me? Saved me? That stupid dog …"

"Stupid? She didn't come out when you hit the barrel with the rake, did she?"

"No, but ..."

"Well, I call that being a very smart dog."

And with that she left me and went out into the garage and brought Lillie back into the house.

Lillie avoided me for a couple days, but one afternoon as I sat reading on the floor with my back against the couch, she came over and sat beside me.

She sat there for a long time not moving, Finally, I stopped reading and looked over at her. Quickly, before I could stop her, she licked my face.

There are a lot of things you can do about someone you love, but staying mad at them is not one of them.

I gave her a great big hug.

THE BUGABEAR

(I wrote this many years ago when we lived in New Orleans. I had been watching my two children stay up past their bedtime and the next day wrote down what I saw. I thought it would be appropriate for Halloween. Remember it's all true but the last sentence and I'm really not too sure about that...)

Mike put the empty iced tea glass carefully down on the tabletop and then turned and watched his smaller sister, Cathy.

He realized that it was too late to get any ice from her; already the last piece from her glass was lumped half in and half out of her mouth. The water drooling down her chin had soiled the top of her nightie.

He quickly went over and took the empty glass she held and put it beside its twin on the table. He knew they had to be careful; the crash of a broken glass would remind their parents that the two of them were still up, and it was well past their already extended bedtime.

He looked again at Cathy. It was no use. The small piece of ice she had had was gone. He wet his lips as he looked at her; he was still thirsty.

"Tice," she said, pointing toward the kitchen.

He looked to where she was pointing and then remembered the ice tray on the kitchen counter beside the sink.

She was right. The tray might still hold some unmelted ice. They would be able to get more. There was a stepstool there and he would be able to reach the tray.

He nodded his head at her and they both hurried through the short hall toward the dark kitchen. When they reached the sill, however, Cathy stopped abruptly.

Mike, right behind her, stopped also. Puzzled, he looked at his sister. Cathy was starring into the kitchen, into the dark.

After a moment, her hand went up and she pointed mysteriously at the room.

She whispered... “Bugabear.”

Mike turned from her and looked into the gloom of the kitchen.

At first he could see nothing; then, as his eyes grew accustomed to the darkness, he began to make out the stool and then the refrigerator hulking, huge and white in the darkness.

He stared long and hard until finally the sink counter and the closet outlines became clearer and more familiar to him.

He started to step over the sill, when he felt that his sister was not with him. Looking back, he saw her squatting on her haunches, her body rocking from side to side as she looked knowingly into the different corners of the room ahead of him.

"Bugabear,"

She had whispered it again.

He stepped back and squatted by her side.

His eyes grew big as he tried to see the whole room. By now his eyes had grown fully accustomed to the dim light, he could see all of the objects in the room.

As he slowly looked from object to object, he licked his lips nervously.

The gloom at the top of the refrigerator, the inside of the sink itself, and beyond these, the far side of the stove -- these he could not see. He listened, straining his ears to tell him the things his eyes could not see.

Suddenly the remaining ice in the tray shifted as it melted, plopping several cubes noisily into the melted portion of the tray.

Cathy stood up quickly and started running, leaving a startled Mike staring into the dark room.

He stood up still staring; his mouth a small "o". And then, turning, he swiftly followed her through the short hall into the well-lighted living room. Here, their hurried entrance, reminded their parents of the time. In moments both children were picked up and carried off to bed.

***

In the kitchen, the electric clock purred quietly on the wall above the rapidly melting ice.

In the deep shadow beside the stove, the Bugabear idly flexed its long claws, stared hungrily at the empty doorway, then sighed and slowly, very slowly, disappeared.

WEEKEND GUESTS AND OTHER FRIENDS

... The other night as I went out to the patio to recover a book I had left out there, I heard a mocking bird sing in the dark of the night. It was a lonely sound of some strong feeling that only the bird knew. Its song went on for a while. He was still singing when I finally turned and went back into the house. ...

We had some visitors that stopped by late last week and stayed for the weekend.

There were two of them, flying in real low and first staying over in Lister's Pond and then, seemingly undecided, going to the small pond just to our east. Finally they seemed to settle on the beach, sauntering for an hour or so up and down the berm just above the high water mark.

We noticed them because they were so noisy. Their back and forth flights just at rooftop height was accompanied by a social chattering of honks, with both birds speaking at once.

The two were Canada Geese. I wondered at their size. They were smaller than the ones I had been used to seeing when I lived years ago in Maryland. I looked them up in our bird books and was surprised to learn that there are several different sizes of Canada Geese. It has to do with racial stock. Our two visitors, it seems, were in a mid-size variety.

These were an interesting pair. They were very busy, seemingly concerned with checking on everything in the local vicinity and discussing each item endlessly.

It turned out they were the advance party of a small group of migrating geese. We noted the arrival of two more birds the morning of the next day, then several more later on, until by Saturday, there were eight Canada Geese enjoying the beach and the two side ponds.

None of the birds seemed to believe in spending any time in quiet meditation. They were in all a noisy, gregarious, happy group and when they left Monday, Stella and I were sorry to see them go.

We get a lot of migratory birds stopping by briefly like that in early spring. The variety is always interesting. Sometimes one kind would visit every year, then for some reason would not return for several years or stop coming at all.

For example, we used to have ducks stop by. A lot of ducks, and these would often stay a week or more. We haven't seen too many the last few years. I do remember, however, that some of the ducks were sometimes rather shocking in their behavior, seemingly more interested in sex rather than migrating.

A lot of this was just several drakes strutting after a hen. But on occasion a drake would get lucky and the pair would run in the bushes behind the house to carry on. You could almost walk up on them; they were so shameless.

Gretal, our Weimaraner at the time, tried to install a certain amount of decorum to their actions by trying to eat them. But they ignored her and flew to the house next door and continued on as before.

Then there are the hummingbirds.

Now, there's a group that appear to be fighters not lovers. Each bird seems to have seen the movie "Top Gun" two or three dozen times and pictures itself in the starring role.

Their endurance is amazing.

They seem to go at each other almost continuously, trying to show their skills at blinding territorial fights around the five or six feeders we have about the house. I get tired just watching them.

I suppose it takes all kinds, but any one humming bird isn't even big enough to make a single kind of anything else.

***

Last year we built a small, enclosed brick patio around the side of the house, away from the wind and beach with its noisy visitors.

It took awhile to get it all finished, what with the easement applications, the cement workers, the brick suppliers and then the brickers themselves. We didn't really get to use it very much before winter set in.

It's still not quite finished. We have some redwood siding to replace which I had been taken down during the construction, but it's essentially done. I have been taking my laptop and sitting back there on occasion this spring when the wind gets too strong on the front porch.

At first I was surprised at the quiet. But then I realized it is not quiet. There are noises, but these are different from what I am used to hearing in the front of the house bordering the beach. I start to hear birds that I know are also around in front but not as noticeable.

Mockingbirds, for example. Normally in front, I see these as birds completely occupied in defending their nests from predators that range from crows to squirrels. If I hear them singing, it's a territorial warning to another mockingbird and the preamble to a whirling series of high speed chases through the tree branches.

Now, however, I hear them singing beautiful airs that rise up and float with an almost unconscious beauty.

No doubt the same songs were sung in front but were dampened by the sounds peculiar to the beach view. Here they are more secluded and they and other land bird songs can be heard and appreciated in their isolation.

The other night as I went out to the patio to recover a book that I had left out there, I heard a mockingbird singing in the dark of the night. It was a lonely sound of some strong feeling that only the bird knew. Its song went on for a while.

He was still singing when I finally turned and went back into the house.

Today, I have gone back to the patio to sit and work. I hear around me the songs of spring. I hear the coo of a dove. This is a wondrous sound! Why had I not heard its inherent soft beauty before?

I find myself putting down the laptop and leaning back on the lounge. Jennie moves beside the lounge, rearranging herself into a more comfortable position. She knows by my actions that we will be here for a while.

Laying on the brick wall, its body stretched out in a long recline, Holly, watches us for a few moments, then closes his eyes and goes to sleep. As soon as he closes his eyes, he ceases to be a tomcat and becomes a long furry duster that had been left by mistake up on the brick wall.

Stella will be home in an hour or so. I might just as well stay here and wait for her.

I close my eyes and join Jennie and Holly in a short nap amid the refreshing noises of a new spring.

WHEN ENOUGH IS ENOUGH

...The new fans had extra long wires. As I moved one to measure what I had to cut off, it crossed both of the old fan's wires. ...There was an extraordinary loud pop and a tremendous flash! ... There was a smell of burnt insulation. ... Lorelei was very quiet. ...

It seems like a long time ago, but I remember the incident quite well.

We were living at the time by a large stand of very old, very tall tulip trees. I say they were tall; many averaged more than one hundred feet in height. Occasionally after a storm, or perhaps from old age, one of the trees would fall and lie to rot on the forest floor.

A walk in the woods would disclose small linear glades where one of these giants had fallen, squashing the smaller trees beneath it and clearing an area when it fell. Soon the surrounding tall trees would send their limbs over the spot and one would find a long, well shaded line on the forest floor full of the humus of the rotten tree.

One spring, my seven-year-old daughter Cathy and I went into the woods to collect some of the tree humus to use in the flowerbeds that surrounded the house we had then.

As we went deeper into the woods, we spotted the trace of a tree that had rotted away completely. There was no humus left, but at the base where the tree had stood a few inches of the old bole could still be seen. It was loaded with a rich humus that evidently went deep into the roots of the tree.

The humus had had a chance to age and deteriorate for several years. It was perfect for what I wanted. I told Cathy this and to get out the bag and we would fill it with humus to take home.

I lay down on the ground and started scooping the material up with a small hand scoop and putting it in the plastic sack Cathy held open for me. We worked in silence for several minutes, Cathy on her knees beside me, pushing the humus deeper in the sack as I brought it out of the ground.

As I got deeper into the bole, I abandoned the scoop and laid down flat on the ground, almost on my face, my arm shoulder-deep in the ground groping with my hand into the roots of the old tree. Cathy moved close beside me, bagging the material as fast as I pulled it out.

Suddenly, I felt something small moving along the arm I had deep in the ground. I stopped moving, my eyes on Cathy, but my mind focused on the thing moving up my arm.

Cathy, seeing my expression, froze.

Then breaking the surface, only inches from my face, was a small snake. A very brightly, multi-colored small snake! Without losing its momentum, it slithered by us and disappeared into the surrounding underbrush.

We stayed unmoving for what seemed like minutes, then Cathy said in a heavy whisper, "I think we have enough humus now, Daddy."

I stayed there for a moment longer, then pulled my arm out of the tree roots and, looking around, agreed with her.

We gathered the few tools we had and tying shut the sack, we went home with what we had.

It was years later before that incident came back to me.

***

We have three ceiling fans on the porch of our present house. Over the years, the three original fans had suffered from the salt spray coming from the Mississippi Sound and all three fans had stopped being of any use.

My granddaughter, Lorelei, was visiting for several weeks one summer and she and I went to Home Depot and bought three new fans to replace the rusted ones, plus an additional one to replace the fan in our gazebo. That fan had also seen better days.

Replacing the porch fans didn't go as quickly as I thought it would. The old fans resisted being taken down by offering stripped screws to unscrew or just becoming impossibly awkward to remove. We kept at it, however, and, by the afternoon of the second day, we had finished two of the three porch fans and had started on the third.

As we worked, I tried to teach Lorelei safety in doing electrical work and emphasized turning off the power before we worked. "Never work with a hot circuit," I said in a running monologue. "You can, but it's needlessly dangerous. Always check and recheck that the power is off and if you are doing the work, turn the power off yourself. That is the only way you can be sure… etc."

I'm sure she found what I was saying repetitious and boring, but I was her Paw Paw and she never hesitated to nod her head agreeably.

When we started on this last porch fans, I checked the power and Lorelei did too. We checked that the fan didn't operate – it didn't – and, satisfied that all was well, started to take this last fan down. The fact that there could be a different circuit powering this fan and that the old fan didn't work even with the power on never occurred to me.

Taking the fan down went rather easy and it looked like its old connection wires could be used for the new fan. I straightened each of these wires out and started putting up the ceiling attachment for the new fan.

"Always act like the wires are hot," I said keeping up my monologue and, from my position on the ladder, motioned Lorelei to hand me up the assembled fan. Lorelei nodded and, climbing up on the first rung helped me hang the fan from a temporary hook in the ceiling so that I could connect the wires.

The new fans had extra long wires. As I moved one to measure what I had to cut off, it crossed both of the old fan's wires.

There was an extraordinary loud pop and a tremendous flash!

I gazed at the scorched wires, realizing what had happened. All about us was the smell of burnt insulation.

Lorelei was very quiet.

"Give me the cutters and the two wire nuts," I said.

She got down and handed these to me and I quickly snipped the new wires the correct length and fastened them with the wire nuts to the old wires. Then with Lorelei's help, I unhooked the fan from its temporary hook and attached it to the ceiling connection plate.

Still on the ladder, I pulled the chain on the fan. It worked perfectly. I looked over at Lorelei and saw the same expression that I had seen on Cathy in the woods those many years ago.

"Can we just skip the gazebo fan for now, Paw Paw?"

I looked over at the gazebo. "Yeah, it really works OK. We really don't have to replace it now." Lorelei nodded and started to help me pick up the trash from our work.

That was two years ago and the gazebo fan has still not been replaced. Maybe when she visits next year.

MAYBE SHE WON'T NOTICE

...What was really eye-catching was the two carved drawers in the very top part of the desk. Their place as well as their carving gave just the right touch to make the piece complete. ...

"Why, Paul, this looks really nice."

I worry when Stella says things like that. We were in the antique mall over in Pass Christian. It was one of those interesting places you like to wander through on a Sunday afternoon and we were doing that. I can normally look at whatever she sees and say agreeably, "Oh yes, that is nice," and move on. But something had definitely caught Stella's eye and I began to worry.

I went over to see what she was admiring. What she was looking at was obviously not an antique, but a newly made ornate mahogany secretary. It did seem rather nice. It was Indonesian and, while ornate, the carving was not overdone.

What was really eye-catching was the two carved drawers in the very top part of the desk. Their place high on the desk, as well as the ach made by their carving gave just the right touch to make the piece complete.

Stella seemed sold and so I discretely looked for the price tag before I made any remarks that would commit me. To my surprise, the price was reasonable.

I smiled.

That was a mistake and in a few moments the mall vendor was writing a receipt for Stella.

"Paul will come by next week with the truck and pick it up," Stella told the woman. At the word "truck" I inwardly cringed. Stella never refers to my 1989 silver Ford Ranger as anything but "the truck." It had to do with a disagreeable incident that occurred when we bought the pickup years ago. The salesman had left her name off the title.

I managed to keep a smile on my face and nodded when the women informed me I would have to come by Tuesday as they were closed on Monday.

The desk wasn't very large, but I asked a friend to help me when I went the following Tuesday. We tied it securely with bungee cord to the eyelets in the side panels of the pickup and I drove carefully home, where Frank and I eased the desk into its assigned place in the master bedroom.

As I stepped back to look at it, however, something seemed wrong. It seemed not to have the presence it had had when Stella and I had first seen it. While it didn't exactly seem bland, it lacked something.

Then it came to me. It was the two top carved drawers! They were missing! The two slots for the drawers had the same varnish finish as the rest so that if you didn't know that they were to hold drawers, you would have thought they were merely slots to hold letters.

"Frank, we lost the drawers on the road! We've got to go back and look for them before someone runs over them!"

Amid Franks protests of, "Are you sure there were drawers there? I don't remember any drawers," "It looked alright to me," "Don't worry about it. She probably won't even know they're gone," and my own equally inane, "She'll kill me, Frank," "What am I going to tell her?" "Keep looking Frank," we slowly drove back along Beach Boulevard looking for the missing drawers.

We had no luck and, as we drove over the long span of the Bay of St. Louis Bridge, it appeared even more hopeless.

First, it was difficult to see over on the opposing lane of bridge traffic and, second, since the traffic was fairly constant, any thought of finding anything left of the drawers but a mass of splinters seemed wishful dreaming.

As we entered the construction area of Henderson Point and started up the new Pass Christian high rise, things became even more complicated. Just as the driver behind us was starting to lean on his horn, irritated at my slow speed, I caught a brief glimpse of dark brown near the concrete shoulder of the opposite lane of the overpass.

Accompanied by Frank's protests, I made a u-turn through the construction area on the other side of the high rise and returned to where I had seen the objects. We parked with caution lights flashing and held up traffic, while I got out and examined the pieces of wood strewn on the shoulder.

It was the drawers.

I was lucky. They were so light they had not been badly damaged. The shock of hitting the concrete at twenty-five miles an hour had caused the drawers to fly apart. But for this and some rather hard gauges and scrapes on their front panels, they were in surprisingly good shape. I picked the pieces up and got back in the pickup.

Now we headed back home accompanied by Frank's "You can glue it back," "Get a little brown paint, she'll never notice the difference," and my own, "She'll kill me," "What'll I tell her? How can I get them fixed?" On the other side of the Bay Bridge, I stopped at a small bookstore and ran inside.

"Susan, you have to help me. Who can I go see to get this fixed?" and I thrust the pieces of the drawers at the startled proprietor. She looked at it for a moment and gave me the name of a friend of hers in the Bay. "I'm sure she can get it fixed, Paul, if anyone can."

When I drove into the Bay and showed it to the woman, she said yes that it was repairable. The gauged areas will be replaced "so you won't even know it was damaged." "Yes, yes," I said anxiously. Then she said, "We'll have it done in about three to four weeks."

"Not this afternoon?" I stuttered.

"Perhaps, two weeks," she said laughing and I left.

I drove slowly back to the house and looked at the desk. Unbelievable as it sounds, without the two top drawers it was just a desk. A very nice desk, but still just a desk.

"I don't know what you're so worried about," Frank said as he stood beside me. "She probably won't even notice it."

That evening when Stella came home and went into the bedroom to change clothes, I heard the yell even in the kitchen. Frank had been wrong. She had noticed.

***

It was two weeks before the woman called me and told me the drawers were repaired. When I picked them up, they looked good. I felt good. When I got home and slipped them into their slots in the top of the desk, they looked perfect.

The woman had been right. You could not tell the drawers had been damaged. In its place in the room, the desk again had the charm it had had when Stella had seen it at the antique mall. I sighed with relief.

When Stella came home that evening and went into the bedroom to change, I stood there waiting for her reaction. She looked at it and turned and smiled at me.

"Why, Paul, this looks really nice."

TIDAL FLATS ON A WINTER DAY

... Jennie, like the ripples, like the snipes, like the clear spotless bright sky above us, is a joy to see, to feel the vibrant life that permeates the entire broad setting in which we are walking. It is, indeed, a wonderful day and we are here, Jennie and I, walking in that wonder. ...

There is a strong winter high today and the wind associated with this atmospheric high has pushed the water four or five hundred feet out from the beach in front of our house.

Highs like this in winter make beautiful days and this is one of the best of those days. This afternoon Jennie, my Weimaraner, and I have taken the opportunity to walk (running in her case) out onto the newly exposed bottom of the Sound.

It's a strange feeling to walk on a surface that is ordinarily covered by the Sound's tea-dark waters. It's as if a plug has been pulled and the floor of the Sound has suddenly been laid bare. One expects to find strange hulks strewn about, relics of some forgotten catastrophe, old ruins, exotic forms.

In a way there are such sights, perhaps not as romantic as man-made debris, but still evidences of the powerful forces that are always at work on the waters of the Sound.

Under my feet as I walk, I see the bottom is corrugated into wave-like ripples an inch or so in height. Spread out in all direction across the exposed bottom, these ripples were formed by the motions of the water when it covered this area during the last tide.

Because of their wave-like appearance, the ripples look as if they are some mud casting of the last tide's sea surface. They are not.

Their beautiful patterns are not direct reflections of what the water's surface once looked like. Rather, their shapes are complex integrations of the many wave motions and other factors. Still, whatever their cause, their distribution about the tidal flat form delightful patterns about me.

As I walk (Jennie is still running), I see that others have been here before us. I see the small trifurcated footprints of several snipes and, looking up, I see the birds themselves are just a few hundred yards ahead of me, walking, flitting about excitedly, looking at these same tidal flats as if they were some smorgasbord of goodies. I suppose to them it is.

A little farther on I see the undeniable imprints of a duck's webbed feet! I have not seen a duck today and looking about still find none. But here at my feet is the undeniable proof that a duck had walked in this same place within the last few hours.

I can't spend any more time looking at these artifacts; Jennie, whizzing by me, grabs my full attention.

She races by in an arc of one of several large elongated circles, whose purpose is sometimes to chase birds and sometimes to make turns that really lead nowhere.

What I see in her passage is the raw release of energy, of letting go after being pent up for too many days. Her paws rip into the mud; leaving clear prints in the rippled bottom that trace the eccentric path she follows in her lopping runs.

Jennie, like the ripples, like the snipes, like the clear spotless bright sky above us, is a joy to see, to feel the vibrant life that permeates the entire broad setting in which we are walking. It is, indeed, a wonderful day and we are here, Jennie and I, walking in that wonder.

***

Yet there are interesting facets to all this.

As I call Jennie and we go back to the house, I see that some action of the receding water has laid a wash of sand that has partially covered some of the rippled bottom.

Peppering the ripples are small holes, filter tubes of fauna that wait the flooding of the next tide. These are also partially covered by the wash of sand. If I carefully scrapped away the sand, I would expose the now covered ripples and the filter holes. But I don't and the area remains covered.

In effect, all of the area covered by the wash had become part of the layer upon layer of material that makes up the subsurface strata of the bottom. Until some tidal current or storm comes along, these features will remain buried in the strata.

With the way the Sound bottom is constantly being worked and reworked by the wind and tidal currents in this area, this will probably happen in a day or so, if not sooner.

But sometimes, in some rare instances, this does not happen and the material stays buried, remaining out of touch of the winds, waves, or tides of our time or even our century.

With this thought, I find myself viewing what I see about me with a different perspective. In my mind's eye I see a sandy outcrop in a narrow canyon in Wyoming that I walked many years ago on a geological field trip.

Deep in the cool shadow of the canyon, I was looking for fossils to give me the geological time of the sediments that composed the tall canyon walls stretching above me toward a distant sky. The chipping of my pick had dislodged a large slab of sandstone and I stared in wonder at the fresh surface that I had bared.

They were ripple marks!

There, exposed by my pick for the first time in hundreds of thousands of years, were the remains of the bottom of a shallow sea.

And imprinted on those ancient ripple marks I could see evidence that something, some prehistoric creature, had run across the exposed bottom of that shallow sea and left a long line of small footprints. Footprints that had kept a clean crisp impression throughout the thousands of years since they had been put down.

That deep canyon I was walking in had once been a broad shallow sea with a bright sun and waves and currents and a tide. During one period of low water, some animal had run on it and left its footprints on the exposed sandy bottom of that sea.

Perhaps in running, it had felt the same sense of joy that I feel on this day as I walk about the tidal flats with Jennie under a crisp clear sky and a bright winter sun.

TRAVEL NOTES

... There are times, however, when there are no friends and a hotel room in Paris on those occasions can be as lonely as any hotel room in a large city...times even with the best of company, you want to be back where your cup of coffee was made by your own coffee machine and the dog that barks at you does so because she wants you to throw her a Frisbee. ...

I guess I'm like anyone else in that I like to travel.

There is something that is more than just pleasant about seeing things that you are not used to seeing. You come away with a new viewpoint; a viewpoint you would not have if you had not had that particular travel experience. And best of all, if friends are involved in the travel, you get the learning experience sugar coated.

For years I worked on a broad study of the Mediterranean Sea. I did this in conjunction with a group of European scientists and had to spend extended periods with several of them in the countries that bordered the sea, especially Spain, France and Italy. I enjoyed my stay in all of these, but I suppose I like Italy the best.

It seems to me that the very essence of Italian society is a subtle style of sophisticated civilization not found in other countries. Basically, it is the realization that the rules of a truly civilized society were made to ease the ability of its people to get along with each other rather than be rules that exist independent of human nature.

I remember once in Naples, being caught in a traffic tie up. Everything had come to a dead halt and promised to stay that way for sometime. Yet I could see that the traffic was clear about a block ahead of me.

Since I was late for an important appointment, I became desperate. I looked around and finding my way clear, drove my car up on the sidewalk in an effort to go around the tie up.

I had not gone but perhaps a half a block along the sidewalk, when I encountered two Italian policemen talking and looking out at the traffic confusion. When they heard me coming, they stopped their conversation and politely stepped to one side to allow me to pass.

Once I got beyond them, I became interested in seeing if they had returned to their private chat. Looking in my rear view mirror, I was surprised to see that they were waving through a number of other cars that had evidently followed me onto the sidewalk.

On another occasion, I had my large briefcase stolen at the train station in Milan. I even saw the thief before he surreptitiously walked off with my bag. I remember that he had a pleasant face like the night porter at my hotel and gave me a nice smile. When I looked again, he was gone and so was my bag.

I was extremely upset. It contained all my work that I had come to Italy to do. I explained everything in endless detail to the railroad police, who told me politely in French (no one spoke English, but my name was French, non?) to maintain my tranquility.

After an hour of this, I found I had missed the express to La Spezia, my destination that day. I was forced to wait several more hours and take a late local. It was extremely slow and it was late in the evening when I finally arrived in La Spezia.

Feeling low I walked in the dusk the short distance to the apartment building of the people I was staying with. When I rang the bell, I was surprised to hear from the lobby intercom, "Paul, is that you? Come up, please we have your briefcase!"

And indeed they did!

The thief in Milan had emptied everything of value from the briefcase and then, going to the delivery entrance of an exclusive shop, rang the bell and ran away, leaving the case on the steps.

The shop's proprietor, rather than call the police, opened the case, found my wife's phone number in Mississippi, and called her. My wife, completely confused about what was taking place, told her where I had planned to stay in Italy.

This was to have been in Rome, but when the women in Milan called the people in Rome, they said that no, I wasn't in Rome, that I had planned to stay overnight with some friends in La Spezia.

The Milan shop owner then called my friends in La Spezia and informed them of what she had found on her doorstep. After finding out that I was indeed due there some time that day, she quickly arranged for the briefcase to be sent to La Spezia on the next train. And when I arrived, the briefcase was there.

I told the story to several of my Italian friends during my stay. None thought what had happened to be unusual.

***

During that several year period when my work required extensive traveling, I tried to take Stella with me on at least one foreign trip a year to ease the pressure my absence made to our marriage. On one trip to Italy (again La Spezia), she couldn't come with me, and I had to go without her.

After spending several days getting the things done that I needed to do, I went with my friends to their weekend place in the hills 40 miles east of the city.

It was a wonderful retreat, removed from all the things that I was normally accustomed to in my everyday life.

My room that night was the upper floor of a small stone house almost a thousand years old. I slept on a straw mattress and was warmed by a fire in the small raised fireplace by the bed. I fell asleep watching the firelight flicker on the stone walls of my small room.

Later that night, I awoke and listened to the night noises around me. Outside my window I could hear a waterfall and a bird that sang to me and the rest of the world through most of the night.

The next morning we had an Italian breakfast of coffee, toast and a piece of fruit and went to the rear of the house to look at my friend Mario's small vineyard. He proudly showed me his several rows of grapes and assured me that if I came back the next fall we would make wine from the grapes using the old wine press under the village church. I actually did go back and we did make wine that year.

At midday we went to the local restaurante/bar and sat in a side room with many of the locals from the tiny village. There were just a few large tables and no real menu. People sat wherever there was room to sit and everyone was served by plates of food that continuously seemed to come out of the kitchen.

Through the room's windows, I could see the valley and the hills on either side. Another small village was perched high on the hill to our right. I knew it was going to be a long meal and relaxed and enjoyed the warm ambiance of good food and wonderful people.

Paola, Mario's wife was upset with me that Stella had not been able to make the trip. She said so to me and also to the people who joined us at our table, and to the restaurante proprietor at the bar as well as the cook in the kitchen (who had learned her English in Scotland and spoke it with a rich Scottish burr).

I sat explaining why Stella wasn't with me for perhaps the tenth time when I heard Paola's voice over the noise in the room, "Stella! How are you?" I looked up to where Paola sat talking on the phone in the far corner of the room.

She had called Stella in Mississippi!!

I quickly got up to go talk to Stella myself, when someone stopped me to say hello. When I looked again, the proprietor had started to talk to Stella explaining something about the menu, then the cook came on to clarify what he had said, then someone that I knew couldn't speak English, started singing to her on the phone an Italian song.

It seemed everyone in the room got to talk to Stella before I did that day.

Later when I returned home, Stella told me about having the wonderful experience of going to bed in Mississippi and waking to the phone ringing and finding herself for a little over a half hour in a small village in the hills of Italy.

***

There are times, however, when there are no friends and a hotel room in Paris on those occasions can be as lonely as any hotel room in a large city.

These are the times that, even with the best of company, you want to be back where your cup of coffee was made by your own coffee machine and the dog that barks at you does so because she wants you to throw her a Frisbee.

I once had a six-month position at a university in Mallorca, Spain. It was a beautiful island and I had been given a car and an apartment one block from the Royal Palace on a quiet walking street beside a postage-sized square. I liked my work and I was given travel funds so that I could travel about the Mediterranean fairly freely.

After three months, Stella joined me for a few weeks. We had a wonderful time. It was in early spring and we made the most of her stay in visiting small obscure places on the island.

On weekends, it became a standing joke between us that we would start off to go to the beach at nine in the morning and not get there till five in the evening.

Then she left to go home and I found myself alone on an island in the Mediterranean thousands of miles from Stella and our home in Mississippi.

After a couple weeks, I went in to sit and talk with my sponsor. "Joaquin," I said after reviewing some work we had done together. "I think I'm going to have to go home."

"But Paul, you still have almost two months to go. Everything is going extremely well. Why do you want to leave? Do you want to go to Barcelona and visit with Jordi for a couple days? We can arrange that very easily."

I explained that I had really done all the work that we had set out to do together, that there really wasn't any more reason to stay, and that my work at my home office was piling up and fax messages were insufficient in letting me catch up (Spain did not have e-mail then).

I said everything to him except the real reason that I just wanted to go home.

I stayed another week and then caught the plane that started my way back to a house on the beach in a small town on the Mississippi Gulf Coast.

In truth, it is nice to travel. But when you get down to it, Dorothy said it best when she clicked her ruby red slippers together and said,

"There's no place like home!
There's no place like home!
There's no place like home!"

YOU HAVE TO TALK THE FISHERMAN TALK, WALK THE FISHERMAN WALK

... "No, not a bit. Lots of bait fish," he said sitting on one of the white plastic chairs I pulled over for him to sit on. "More bait fish than I've ever seen before. All over the place. But nothing else. Maybe it's the salt keeping everything back in the river and Bayous." ... I leaned back in the lounge. It had started. They had begun the talk, the fisherman talk. ...

We were sitting on the small wooden deck besides the porch that somehow always catches a breeze. Today, there was just the soft breath of a breeze, just enough to make things pleasant.

Stella was in the hammock and I was stretched out on the lounge. It was one of those rare Saturdays when Stella and I had been able to do all the chores that we had set out to do and were killing the little time left before lunch.

I was comfortable and had dropped my arm so that I could reassuringly touch the sun-warmed back of Jennie sleeping on the deck beside my lounge. She had been twitching in her sleep, chasing something down the secret passages of her mind.

I was debating on whether to turn on my right or left side when I happened to glance out toward Carrere's pier. I could see the small figure of a fisherman slowly heading back to the beach, casting his line inside the pier's poles as he walked through the shallows.

"Looks like someone's been trying their luck on the rising tide," I said to Stella who immediately sat up and looked toward the pier.

"Maybe he's having a little better luck than I've been having," she said ruefully watching the fisherman's slow progress for a few moments and then laying back on the hammock.

Yesterday was one of those alternate Fridays Stella has off from work. She had gotten up before daybreak and had gone over by that same pier to wade fish. She had stayed out till after ten and then returned disgusted with only two fish, a Black Drum and a Speckled Trout.

They were small; barely lunch size. They were the size that makes you have to fill the spaces in your tummy with lots of lettuce and tomatoes. Luckily the tomatoes are extra sweet this year and we did have a good lunch.

Now, as I watched her, I could tell she was going over in her mind the poor luck she had been having fishing. After twenty-five years, I had no trouble following her chain of thought. I knew her next thought would be whether it would have been worth getting up this morning and going fishing rather than what she had actually done: make me a batch of vanilla ice cream and some Boursin cheese spread.

While the Boursin was lagniappe, I consider both ice cream and fresh fish part of life's essentials. I was of two minds on the options that I knew were the next step in Stella's thinking on how she should spend the rest of the weekend.

Behind me, I heard a pickup pull over and stop on our side street and its door open and slam shut. Stella looked up and immediately sat up straight. I sat up also and saw walking toward us the brother of a neighbor that lives up the street. He lives in north Mississippi, but since he's an ardent fisherman, he often came down to the coast and spends a few days at his sister's so that he can wade fish in the Sound.

As he approached, I noticed two things. The first was that the short rubber boots he had on made a squashing noise as he walked and the second was that he was the fellow I had seen over by Carrere's Pier.

"Did you have any luck," both Stella and I asked as one.

"No, not a bit. Lots of bait fish," he said sitting on one of the white plastic chairs I pulled over for him to sit on. "More bait fish than I've ever seen before. They were all over the place. But there weren't anything else. Maybe it's the salt keeping everything back in the rivers and bayous."

I leaned back in the lounge. It had started. They had begun the talk, the fisherman talk.

Stella started asking him what he using to fish with, shrimp or lures and then what kind of lures (she has an artificial lure called "Top Dog" and when she goes out wade fishing she sometimes says she's "walking the dog").

I've been the third wheel on too many of these conversations to think it would be anything different. I sat politely, fighting to keep a glazed look from coming across my face. I even managed to ask an intelligent question or two to keep up an appearance of at least some attention.

It really didn't matter; Stella was in her element talking animatedly about something that was really important to someone who felt the same way. Whatever I said would have been fine. I sat and just let the two of them talk.

I began to drift away, watching the water and only half listening to their conversation. The wind had picked up slightly and a few white caps had started to appear on the water. I saw a pelican and then, further away, another pelican fishing very low over the water. There were no others. Maybe the fishing was as bad as the two of them were saying. Away to our west, a clump of shrimp boats was working an area of the Sound that evidently had some shrimp.

After a bit, I noticed a change in the tempo of their conversation and quickly tuned back to listening to what they were saying. Our friend was easing himself up from his chair. "Well, I've had it," he said standing. "I'm going to head on back up country this afternoon. Be back toward the end of the month and give it another go."

We talked for a few more minutes and then he headed to his pick up, his boots making squashing noises as he walked.

"Well, that was nice," said Stella watching him drive off. I was about to say something to the effect that, considering his luck, it had been a good thing she hadn't gone out, when I caught myself.

"Yes, it was nice."

We sat there and relaxed for a while longer. I thought about lunch, idly tossing several ideas about what would be nice to have. When I turned to say something on this to Stella, I saw that she was far away, still fishing with our friend.

I settled back, it would be a little longer before lunch.

One Penny, Two Penny, Three Penny, Four ...[*]

...Later that same afternoon, I went to my bank that was luckily open on Saturdays, and stood in a long line to change my pennies to four one-dollar bills. These I stuck separate from the other bills in my wallet. They were a secret trove. ...

For several years after my divorce, my daughter would come to my apartment on weekends, usually a Saturday, and tell me about her week and just talk.

Mind you, what I am talking about took place a long time ago and my daughter is now married with her own grown children. But then it was just the two of us. A dad listening to the important news of his teenage daughter. It was fun.

One rainy Saturday, I pulled out a mayonnaise jar loaded with pennies that I had been saving for more than a year. It was pretty full and as we talked, we occupied ourselves counting the hundreds of coins.

The counting didn't go as quickly as I thought it would. We would each make errors or forget where we started, then argue about whose fault it was and have to start all over again.

We did this several times.

---

[*] Printed in *The Sea Coast Echo* on December 5 1999, just before our twenty-fourth wedding anniversary

It didn't really matter; it passed the morning beautifully. Especially when we had to get in the car and drive through the rain looking for a store that had coin wrappers. Finally we finished counting and rolling the pennies and I found to my surprise that I had accumulated all of $8.35.

Remember, this was a long time ago, actually almost twenty-five years. It was a time when $8.35 was still a nice amount of money, even if that amount was made up of hundreds of pennies.

After mentally patting myself on the back for my thrift, my daughter and I split the rolls between us; she took four dollars and I kept four dollars, putting the 35 cents back in the mayonnaise jar as seed money for more pennies.

I prepared lunch for the both of us and we talked some more. But I could see in her eyes that she was imagining all the things her half of the count could buy. We quickly finished lunch and I kissed her good bye and let her go. We had other Saturdays after that, but that was a fun one that I remember well.

Later that same afternoon, I went to my bank that was luckily open on Saturdays, and stood in a long slow-moving line to change my pennies to four crisp one-dollar bills. These I stuck separate from the other bills in my wallet. They were to be a secret trove.

That night, I took a rather special date to a nice restaurant and found we had to wait in the bar for our table. I ordered two glasses of wine and we talked. As I said, she was a special person and we had a very pleasant talk. After a bit, the hostess came in and told us our table was ready.

As we rose to follow her, I signaled the bartender for our tab.

"Don't worry about it, sir," he said moving on to another customer. "I'll have it added to your dinner bill."

I was about to turn and leave when I remembered the bills in my wallet from all those saved pennies. I pulled out my wallet, and waved him back.

"Let me go ahead and pay."

He gave me the tab. When I looked at the amount, I found it was for exactly four dollars. I paused, staring at the tab. A year of saving pennies and all I got was two glasses of wine! I slowly pulled the bills out from my wallet where I had hid them and laid them on the bar. Then, remembering that that didn't include the tip, I added an extra dollar.

I turned from the bar and went to where my date was waiting.

"How was the wine?" I asked impulsively.

"It was very, very nice" she said and took my arm and, as we followed the hostess to our table, she smiled at me.

It was a beautiful smile.

As I said, that was almost twenty-five years ago. On December 13 of this year, we celebrate our twenty-fourth wedding anniversary. Her smile is still beautiful.

I'm starting to save my pennies. I'm going to take her out to dinner in December of next year and buy her another glass of wine.

It will be a special glass, bought by a special trove of memories.

DOING SEVENTY[*]

Salud ! !

This is my big year. In April of this year, I will be seventy.

I've been waiting for this. Being seventy years old always seemed to me to be some unattainable summit, like some distant Himalayan peak, something I could see in the distance, but only faintly. I could see it getting closer, but never really believing I would see it up this close.

Now it's no longer a distant sight, it's here. Or almost here. I've jumped the gun a little bit. Within a week after my sixty-ninth birthday, I started to answer questions about my age with a stock answer, "I'll be seventy on my next birthday." This way I've managed to drag out the feeling of being seventy almost a full year before it actually takes place.

On my birthday in April of this new year, when I do turn seventy by the count, I'll start dragging it out in reverse, "I turned seventy on my last birthday." I'll keep this up till I reach seventy-one, in effect making myself seventy for two years. Well heck, it's my seventy and, by golly, I'm going to enjoy it.

I've had other memorable birthdays. When I turned eighteen and could enter the service in time for the occupation of Europe and the Korean War.

---

[*] Published in the *Sea Coast Echo* on January 2, 2000

When I was twenty-one, when I was stuck in a backwater military base in Cuba. When I was thirty, when I was in college full time, working twenty hours a week with a wife and two kids. Looking back, these supposed milestone years don't seem to have been too exciting.

On my sixtieth birthday, however, I was in my prime. Or at least I felt like I was. When someone asked how old I was, I would say that I was "a sixty- year-old man with a forty-year-old boy inside trying to get out."

The truth was that I didn't want to be sixty. Sixty was old and I didn't feel old.

To prove this, I ran a ten-kilometer race on my sixtieth birthday. Luckily, I was accompanied by two good friends who were skirting their early forties. They paced alongside of me, carrying on a conversation that only required my grunting a "yes" or a "no."

As we drew to the finish line, it became obvious to us that we were coming in last. All of the other runners had long since finished the race.

But as we got closer, we could see that most of the runners had stayed at the finish line. They were yelling, yelling for me to "come on!" This included my wife Stella, who I could see standing ahead of the crowd and yelling the loudest.

I pushed and tried my best to "come on!" There was a burst of the considerably small amount of energy I had in me and, lo and behold, I finished.

I gasped and gasped and tried to apologize to Stella for finishing last. She and everyone around us laughed. It seemed that as the three of us approached the finish line, my two friends had fallen back in deference to me and had crossed the line together, tying for last place.

Well, on my seventieth birthday, I'm not running any races. I think I've run all my races. I don't need to try my best to get someplace; I'm already there!

And I love it.

I love getting up in the morning and greeting a new day with all the unknowns that it has waiting for me.

I love kissing my wife good night at bedtime and sleeping on a comfortable bed in my own house.

I love the spring with its new life and the fall with its beautiful celebration of that life.

I love the winter with its long sleep and silent promises of tomorrow and the summer with its relaxed blatant enjoyment of today.

I love the wonder of things and the knowledge that everything I have learned so far is just preparation for understanding and appreciating these wonders.

I love to sit by my dog and see her turn her head slightly and look back at me.

I love the colors and sounds of the day and the smell of good food and being tired after doing hard work.

I love lying back and looking up into the amazing symmetry that tree limbs make with the sky and moving clouds.

I love the strong beauty of a dark sky in the far, far distance over the water and in that sky the flash of equally far away lightning and the sound of soft muted thunder.

I love the mystery of seeing something I don't understand and knowing there is even more of that ahead of me. Much more.

I love that there are years ahead of me to enjoy all this and feel that my seventy years were just a start to what lies ahead of me today.

I love the fact that being sixty is years and years behind me and eighty is still a good ways up ahead.

I'm going to stick around and enjoy what I have today. Come on back with me to the kitchen. I think Stella has just made some really good pound cake. Fluffy and light, you'll like it. We'll have it topped with a little dab of whipped cream, some Gran Mariner and we'll toast a great year.

Salud ! !

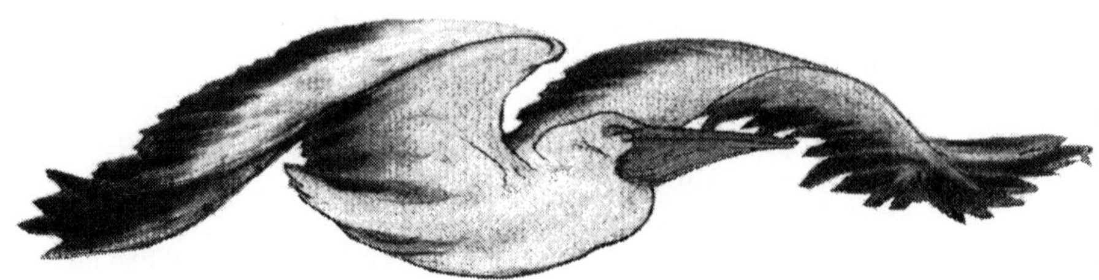

ABOUT THE AUTHOR

Paul Estronza La Violette has been an oceanographer for almost forty years with the government, Mississippi State University and more recently as a consultant with his own company.

He has done his marine research aboard research aircraft and ships in almost all of the world's oceans, spending most of his time in the Arctic Ocean, the Mediterranean Sea and, more recently, the Gulf of Mexico.

His past publications have been oceanographic atlases, books and papers on the circulation of the world oceans and seas. *Waiting For The White Pelicans* is his second non-scientific publication.

He is currently working on a third book: *A Meeting Place Of Waters: The Waters, Lands, Fauna And People Of The Mississippi Sound.* This is scheduled to be published by Annabelle Publishing in the fall of 2001.

He lives on a beach road in Waveland, Mississippi, with his wife, Stella, their dog, Jennie, and a black tomcat named Holly.

IF YOU LIKED THIS BOOK ....

YOU'LL LIKE:

Views from a Front Porch
Living in a Beach House on the
Mississippi Gulf Coast
Paul Estronza La Violette
Illustrated by Stig Marcussen
Waveland, Mississippi